**"Want me, Katie," Cole said fiercely.
"Want me!"**

He wanted her, with an elemental hunger, man for woman. It was plain old desire, primitive and uncomplicated. He wanted her just like this, with nothing between them and the earth but animal skins, nothing over their heads but the sky. He wanted to fill his hands with the textures of her, his mouth with the taste of her, with the sun burning his back and the breeze cooling his sweat.

And he knew she wanted him, too. It was in her eyes, in the heat of her skin beneath his fingers, and in the shudder of wanting she could not disguise.

He cradled her body in his arms and gazed down at her face. "Katie," he murmured, his voice all unanswered yearning and unbridled need.

"Yes," she answered, and drew him to her. "Yes. . . ."

WHAT ARE *LOVESWEPT* ROMANCES?

They are stories of true romance and touching emotion. We believe those two very important ingredients are constants in our highly sensual and very believable stories in the *LOVESWEPT* line. Our goal is to give you, the reader, stories of consistently high quality that may sometimes make you laugh, sometimes make you cry, but are always fresh and creative and contain many delightful surprises within their pages.

Most romance fans read an enormous number of books. Those they truly love, they keep. Others may be traded with friends and soon forgotten. We hope that each *LOVESWEPT* romance will be a treasure—a "keeper." We will always try to publish

LOVE STORIES YOU'LL NEVER FORGET
BY AUTHORS YOU'LL ALWAYS REMEMBER

The Editors

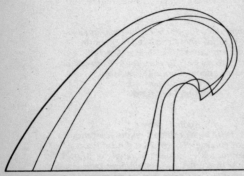

LOVESWEPT® • 208
Kathleen Creighton
Katie's Hero

 BANTAM BOOKS
TORONTO • NEW YORK • LONDON • SYDNEY • AUCKLAND

KATIE'S HERO
A Bantam Book / September 1987

ISBN 0-553-21837-9

PRINTED IN THE UNITED STATES OF AMERICA

O   0 9 8 7 6 5 4 3 2 1

This is for you, my special friend,
for all the gifts you've given me;
but most of all for saying,
when I needed it most,
that a 450 SL was "*me.*"

One

Katherine Taylor Winslow, reigning queen of American romance, wiped sweat from her forehead and stared in disbelief at the mud on her fingers.

If she survived this, she thought, she was going to commit murder.

At the top of her hit list would be the demented genius in the publicity department at Barton and Lord whose brilliant idea this was. Following closely would be Katie's own agent, Sonya Wyatt, for going along with it. After that—well, after that it would have to be Cole Grayson himself, and that would present a problem. Even Katie had to concede that she couldn't just go and bump off the man who was possibly the last honest-to-goodness white-hat hero in America!

"Whoa, horse," she muttered, and was so astonished when the beast she was riding actually obeyed her command that she was caught off balance and bumped an especially sensitive part of her anatomy on the saddle horn. She gasped, "*Ouch!*" then swore bitterly.

The man on the horse ahead of her turned to look

back, and pulled up, grinning. "Ain't much farther now, ma'am," he assured her in a friendly drawl. "I think they're workin' cattle at Blue Meadow today, right on the other side of this ridge."

Katie straightened herself gamely and bestowed a look of martyred dignity upon her guide. She had already discovered that he had a tendency to refer to any geographical formation smaller than the Continental Divide as a "ridge." An interesting fellow, her guide; he'd told her his name was Snake, but hadn't explained why. He was a very thin man, who sat in his saddle in the same boneless slouch whether the horses were proceeding at a shamble, a bone-crunching trot, or a suicidal gallop. The part of his face not covered by a sweat-stained hat and a quarter-inch of beard stubble was leathery; the wisps of hair beneath the hat were the color of dust. His age? A well-preserved sixty or so, she guessed . . . then guessed again. In reality the man was probably not a day over twenty-five.

Katie sank deeper into gloom. This high-altitude California sun was undoubtedly doing to her skin what it had done to his, and she wished she'd yielded and worn a hat. *Oh, Katie—what have you gotten yourself into?* she wondered.

What *was* Katherine Taylor Winslow doing on a jugheaded, razor-backed buckskin cow horse, on her way to a high Sierra cattle drive? *The* K. T. Winslow, dedicated city person, whose idea of high western adventure was shopping on Rodeo Drive! Had all her carefully crafted poise and polish come only to this?

In the final analysis, of course, she knew perfectly well she had no one to blame but herself. Greed, that was what it boiled down to. Greed, pure and simple. Not for money—her poor tax man was probably having a heart attack over her last royalty statement at this very moment. No, Katie's greed involved something more complex and infinitely more rare than money: *heroes.*

Katie was a sucker for heroes; she invariably fell

wildly in love with the ones she created for her books. There was, she acknowledged sadly, a dearth of heroes in the world these days. Oh, she knew that real-life heroes came in all shapes and sizes; that the *real* heroes were the men who trudged off to work in the morning even when they didn't feel like it, who got up without being asked when the baby cried at three in the morning. Sure. But she'd already been through all that, and had reached an age of nostalgic yearnings some people—not Katie!—insisted on calling "middle." What she yearned for were the old-fashioned heroes, heroes who looked like heroes, acted like heroes. Where in this day and age were the heroes played by the Errol Flynns, the Clark Gables, the Gary Coopers? Men with dash and charm, high ideals and intestinal fortitude, men with smoldering eyes, arrogant smiles, strong bodies, and gentle hands, men who could put the fire of passion in a woman's blood or the chill of fear in a man's heart with a look?

Heroes. Oh, yes, as K. T. Winslow she had created them by the dozen, all shapes, sizes, and colors, and she'd adored every single one of them; but she'd never in her life met a man she considered a genuine, flesh-and-blood hero. Presented with the chance to do so, she had found it irresistible.

Cole Grayson. He'd been called the Last Swashbuckler, rightful heir to Flynn's sword and Gable's grin, an eighteenth-century man in a twentieth-century world. His name was box-office gold; he'd never made an unsuccessful movie. Small wonder. He chose his projects carefully, and with faultless timing, and between pictures retired to his mountaintop, leaving the world hungry for more and thirsty for knowledge about the enigma known as Cole Grayson.

Just who the real Cole Grayson was and what he was like were things the public—including Katie—had been wondering for years. Now, with any luck at all, Katie and the public were both going to find out. Heaven only knew why Grayson had agreed to let her write his biography, when he'd steadfastly refused so many other offers. Maybe he was just tired of all the lies, half-truths, rumors, and wild speculations that had been postulated about him through the years. Maybe the idea of having the queen of romantic fiction write the life story of the king of romantic heroes appealed to some latent sense of humor in the man. Did even heaven know? Katie decided she couldn't have cared less. He'd agreed to let her do it, and that was all that mattered.

This opportunity represented a lot more than a chance to interview a charismatic superstar, and she knew it. It was proof positive that she'd reached the top of the heap, something she still had trouble believing most of the time. It was hard to convince herself that she really was K. T. Winslow, sophisticated, elegant world traveler and household name, when just six years ago she'd been plain Kate Winslow, newly divorced and terrified at beginning a new life, a new career. The twins had been starting high school, and all three of them had gone through adolescence together, facing the same giddy, exhilarating roller-coaster ride into an unknown full of wonderful possibilities and frightening pitfalls.

And they'd made it, all three of them. The twins were in college, and she . . . well, she'd already achieved a degree of success and independence that exceeded all the goals she'd set for herself. This project would be the cherry on top of the hot fudge sundae of her life!

She shifted in the saddle, trying to stretch the knots out of her abused muscles, wincing anew at the sting of chafed flesh. It was all going to be worth it, she vowed, gritting her teeth. Every ache, every pain, every inconvenience.

She'd meet the man in hell itself, if those were his terms. Legends, she acknowledged, must be humored.

As she had feared, Snake's "ridge" was another mountain, every bit as steep as the other ninety-nine or so they had traversed since leaving the trucks early that morning. And like all steep hills, what appeared to be its summit was a mirage that kept retreating, like the end of a rainbow. Except that, unlike a rainbow's end, with perseverance, one eventually does come to the top of a mountain. At the summit, Katie's guide halted and pointed.

"There they are."

Katie's horse stopped, too, without any instructions from her. Without being consciously aware of it, her mind shifted into paragraph form, painting the scene spread out before her in descriptive prose.

. . . It was a scene from a John Huston movie; a Charles Russell painting come to life: a sea of grass, dun-colored, sun-gilded, shimmering in heat waves, trampled and bruised beneath the hooves of wild-eyed cattle. Brown horses and brown men seemed as one, like centaurs; and over everything, a golden mist rose, a pall of dust. . . .

Dear Lord, they still do this? Katie asked herself, for one moment wondering if it could be a scene staged just for her benefit.

But no—for all its primitive beauty, the activity in the meadow had the gritty, smelly aura of reality. As she followed her guide's loose-jointed form down the slope, Katie could smell the stench of singed hair mixed with woodsmoke, hear the bawling of the cattle, the slap of leather on leather, the jingle of spurs, the high yips and guttural cries of the working cowboys.

"Which one is Cole Grayson?" she asked Snake.

He gave her a sideways look. "Cain't hardly miss him." He made "cain't" rhyme with "faint." "He's ridin' that big black."

Katie hardly heard him. She was watching one of the cowboys detach himself from the milling herd and gallop toward them, trailing his own dust cloud. Except for the fact that he was mounted on a tall black horse instead of a short brown one, he looked pretty much like everybody else. Until he got closer.

Oh, dear, Katie thought; how in the world do I reduce *him* to words on a piece of paper?

Of course she knew every bone, every line, every wrinkle in his famous face. She knew the color of his hair—brown—and of his eyes—hazel. She knew the shape of his smile, the set of his ears, and the fact that his nose had a slight hook. But she'd purposely tried not to describe him in words, even in her own mind. She'd wanted to meet him with her mind open, a blank page. Now she thought that might have been a mistake. Words were never going to capture whatever it was that made Cole Grayson so devastatingly attractive.

To her dismay, Katie discoverd that her heart was in full gallop. In contrast, the man she had ridden through hell to see seemed perfectly relaxed and at ease, leaning on the pommel of his saddle. He had halted a short distance off and was watching her approach from under the brim of a dusty gray hat, regarding her with the fiercely challenging stare of an annoyed eagle. She had to resist an impulse to lift her hand to her hair in an automatic gesture of feminine self-consciousness she thought she had put far behind her; instead she wiped her palm nervously on her thigh.

Cole Grayson's eyes glowed and flared like live coals. They were, Katie noticed, more topaz than hazel, and the closer she got to him the more he reminded her of an eagle. She felt vulnerable and unprotected, and glanced around, looking for her guide—some sort of buffer, or go-between. But the wretched man had deserted her; he'd dropped back and was sitting on his horse in a placid slouch, toying with the reins and leaving her to face the great Grayson all alone.

She took a deep, fortifying breath and told herself to grow up. She told herself that he was only an actor, after all—a make-believe hero, and no more real than the ones she created with words. She told herself that he was a man. Just . . . a man.

Their horses were nose to nose when Cole Grayson finally spoke, in a voice like the crack of a bullwhip.

"Woman, where in the *hell* is your hat?"

Katie sat in shocked silence for a moment. But speechlessness was a condition she was rarely afflicted with, and never for long. Calm settled upon her. Gazing into those terrible eyes she tilted her head to one side and crisply rejoined, "Not a bad opening line—though I think I've written better."

Did she imagine the spark of surprise in the famous eyes? They flicked sideways to where Snake sat draped over his saddle like a pile of ancient rags. Snake only shrugged, firmly refusing responsibility for Katie's bareheadedness.

Cole shook his head and muttered something under his breath. Katie caught the word "redhead."

The temper usually associated with coloring like hers began to assert itself. It occurred to her that if she didn't establish herself firmly on equal footing with this man right now, she never would, and if she didn't, working with him would be impossible. So, in carefully austere tones, she said, "My hair is auburn, not red. And please don't concern yourself about me. I do not burn or freckle."

But then, why were her face, neck, and arms suddenly burning hot? Cole was giving what he could see of her skin a lazy but thorough once-over, and it was as if his eyes, and not the sun, had scorched where they'd touched her.

"It's not your hide that worries me," Cole drawled. "This high-altitude sun'll turn your brains to mush, don't you know that?"

Well, Katie guessed that explained it. . . . There was a logical reason for the way her heart was beating, for feeling so queasy and light-headed. Thank goodness it was only the altitude!

A smile was tugging at Cole's lips. Katie caught the ghost of a familiar dimple. ". . . Can't have that happen, not if you're going to be writing my life story. We're gonna have to find you a hat."

"That isn't necessary," Katie insisted, pulling herself as straight and tall in her saddle as her stiff muscles would allow. Damn the man—so what if he was famous! So, by God, was she! "I never," she stated with finality, "wear hats."

From Snake's direction, off to her left somewhere, came a sound that might have been a snicker. Cole's eyes zeroed in on hers with all the weight of his personality behind them. Katie braced herself as if meeting physical force, and managed to hold her own gaze steady. With her eyes locked in that golden tractor beam she never saw Cole signal his big black horse, but suddenly he was moving. Moving up alongside her own scrawny buckskin. Her knee brushed his thigh. Without letting go of her eyes he swept the dusty, sweaty hat from his own head and plunked it firmly onto hers.

"Now you do," he said with a verbal economy worthy of Gary Cooper. And then, leaning closer, he added softly but with unassailable authority, "Around here, lady, you wear a hat . . . or you turn around and go back where you came from."

He turned away then, releasing her so abruptly, she felt as though the world had tilted.

Over his shoulder he said to Snake, "If she decides to stay, take her on to camp. Tell Birdie to tend to her." Without another word, without even so much as a glance, a wave, or a "see you later," he wheeled the black horse and headed back to the milling herd at an easy, graceful lope.

Katie realized that her mouth was hanging open, and abruptly closed it. When her horse suddenly came to life and fell into step behind Snake's, she had to clutch at the horn to keep from toppling out of the saddle.

Altitude, she told herself grimly, explaining away the wave of dizziness that had just come over her. Altitude, and sheer, unadulterated outrage. *Just who the hell did he think he was, talking to her like . . . like—*

Suddenly and right out loud, Katie laughed. Snake glanced back at her to see if she had lost her mind or succumbed to the high-altitude sun. Reassured, he grinned, shook his head, and shambled on.

Well, of course, Katie thought with satisfaction. The arrogance, the lazer-beam eyes, the charisma so thick you could plow it—hero stuff, right out of the pages of one of her own books. Or the screenplay from one of Cole Grayson's movies. Perfect. Absolutely perfect.

Well . . . maybe. As her horse plodded patiently along, following Snake's boneless form without any guidance from Katie, she felt her own sweat begin to mingle with Cole's under the weight of his filthy hat, and she found herself frowning. It was occurring to her that the qualities that make a terrific make-believe romantic hero might be somewhat less appealing in a real, flesh-and-blood man.

Cole Grayson, returning to the roundup minus his favorite hat, was smiling. He'd found the encounter with his proposed biographer unexpectedly stimulating. She certainly wasn't what he'd expected. Though he wasn't sure what he *had* expected. Hell, he was still wondering what had made him agree to the deal in the first place. His agent had caught him in a weak moment. He seemed to recall that it had been right around March or April, so no doubt he'd been thinking about Mia. He usually thought about her quite a bit in the spring.

Well, he meant to go through with it—he'd never gone back on his word yet—but to be honest, he'd hoped that by making it tough for her . . . Oh, well. So Katherine Taylor Winslow had turned out to be tougher than he'd expected. She'd turned out to be quite a few things he hadn't expected.

Older, for one thing—might even be close to his own age, though only someone who knew the little telltale things to look for would put her age at much past thirty. Better-looking, too; a lot prettier than the picture on the back cover of her books. Too tall and skinny for his own tastes, of course, but those studio black-and-whites hadn't even hinted at that red—auburn!—hair, or the intelligence in those gray eyes. That was what surprised and pleased him the most. She was sharp, quick with a comeback, and, more important, she didn't seem the least bit intimidated by him. Women usually tended to freeze up and become catatonic in his presence, or so sexy-flirty it made his teeth ache. It had been a long time since he'd had an attractive woman talk to him the way K. T. Winslow just had done.

He considered the possibility that she wasn't susceptible to men at all, and then dismissed it. He had good instincts for things like that. And if he remembered her bio right, she was divorced and had a couple of kids.

On the fringes of the herd he reined in Diablo and turned to look back. Snake and the lady were disappearing into the timber at the far end of the meadow. Even from this distance Cole could see that she was still wearing his hat. He grinned and raked his fingers through his hair, letting the breeze dry his sweat. Then, as a yearling calf made a break for freedom, he dug his heels into Diablo's sides, shouted "Yah!" and took off in pursuit.

Cole Grayson's base camp was nestled on a slope overlooking a beautiful little jewel of a meadow. Unlike the big meadow where the roundup was being held, this one looked lush and green. It was dotted with lupines and sunflowers, and Katie could see flashes of blue sky reflected in the creek that wandered through it.

She and Snake came upon the campsite from above, halting at some corrals in the shelter of a stand of yellow pine. Smoke from a chimney at one end of a long, open-sided building with a tin roof drifted up to them, carrying with it the pungent aroma of chili and roasting meat. The smell made Katie feel nauseated.

"That's the cookhouse," Snake offered, pointing. "And over there's the storehouse, and the cook's cabin. Down below—see where it's green?—that there's the spring. Runs right on down into the creek."

Katie listened politely, but all she wanted in the world right now was a drink of water and to get off that damn horse, not necessarily in that order. For the last half hour or so a whole herd of large animals had been gallumping around inside her skull, and her throat felt as if it had been glued shut.

"Ma'am, why don't you go on down to the cookhouse? I'll see to the horses." Snake's voice was unexpectedly kind. He had dismounted and was standing at Katie's horse's head, holding the bridle and watching her, waiting, presumably, for her to do likewise.

Katie stared back at him. Now that the moment had arrived for her to get off the wretched animal, she wasn't sure she could. Her legs had conformed to the shape of the saddle. If she did somehow succeed in dismounting, she might not be able to walk.

Snake chuckled and flashed a grin that cracked his leathery face in all directions. "Hang on there a minute— I gotcha." He reached up to grip her waist in amazingly strong hands. Katie gave a surprised whoop and found herself standing on the ground.

Which for some reason seemed to be undulating beneath her feet, with a rhythm a lot like the walking gait of a horse. And then there was the kettle drummer— the one who was displaying such remarkable virtuosity inside her head. She groaned, and clutched at Snake's wiry forearms.

"You okay, ma'am?" The cowboy's voice sounded concerned.

Katie squinted at him. Something was wrong with her eyes—he seemed furry. *Damn.* She needed her glasses. Where in the devil were they? Oh, right—they were in her luggage. Where the devil was her luggage?

"Thirsty," she muttered, frowning.

"Birdie'll have something cold—probably got lemonade all made; she always does. She'll give you some liniment, too, I reckon, if you ask her." Snake turned her in the general direction of the camp and gave her an encouraging push, adding helpfully, "Just walk it off, ma'am. You'll get used to it." His chuckle followed her down the slope.

Katie had never considered herself vain, but she did admit to an overabundance of pride. And she was suddenly very, very glad that Cole Grayson wasn't there to witness her painful progress down that hill. She could just imagine what she looked like. Every muscle in her body hurt, and with every step the stiff denim of her pants legs rubbed like sandpaper over the sore places on the insides of her knees. Her head was throbbing, she was nauseated, and she was thirstier than she could ever remember being in her life.

By the time she reached the cookhouse, the world had begun to darken ominously around the edges. In the doorway, she had to brace herself upright with one hand against the rough log frame. She stood blinking into the gloom, trying to focus on the scene before her. She thought dismally that she was hallucinating. It figured.

This end of the shed was enclosed with the same corrugated tin that covered the roof; half filling the enclosed space was a cast iron cookstove the size of a concert-grand piano. And standing in front of the stove was the largest woman Katie had ever seen—not just fat, but tall, at least six feet, with forearms as big around as Katie's thighs. At the moment, one of those massive appendages was raised aloft, holding a huge iron skillet like a tomahawk.

"*Who's that?*" The voice was incongruously high-pitched.

No hallucination, then. Katie realized belatedly that she must be no more than an anonymous silhouette in the doorway, an unexpected and frightening intrusion. She took one step into the cookshed and ventured, "Are you . . . B-Birdie?"

The frying pan came down an inch or so. "Who's askin'?" The woman had a broad face, with the wide, flat cheekbones and slightly Oriental eyes of a Native American. Her hair was salt-and-pepper gray; it crowned her head with a coronet of braids as thick as a man's wrist.

Katie dragged Cole's hat from her own head. "I'm Katherine Winslow. I'm here—"

"My Lord, it's the writer!" The frying pan met the top of the cookstove with a clang that resounded through Katie's head like a Chinese gong. Birdie began to move toward her, only to Katie it was as if the cook were slowly inflating, like a rubber life raft.

What in the world was the matter with her eyes? In an effort to adjust her warped vision, Katie shook her head, but the motion only set off the kettle drummer again.

"You're so tall I thought you was a man," Birdie was explaining in her high, rapid voice. "Some strange man—in those Levis and that hat . . . you never know *who* might come walkin' in these days, with all the crazy dirt bikers and ATC-ers around, tearing up the meadows! Hope I didn't scare you, but with the menfolks gone all day, honey, I'd just as soon be too careful, know what I mean?"

Katie nodded. Birdie had taken her by the arm and was tugging her into the shed's cool and wonderful dimness. "Come on—sit down here, honey. You must be worn out, comin' here on horseback. Now, why you didn't come in on the chopper along with the luggage—"

"Could I please have a drink of water?" Katie whispered, interrupting while she was still capable of speech. In another moment she was surely going to be sick. She'd never felt so awful.

"That's Cole's old hat!" Birdie squinted at it and then leaned over to peer into Katie's face.

Katie gulped. "Yes. He gave it to me. I didn't have one. He seemed to think—"

"You come up here on horseback without a *hat*?"

The cook's hands suddenly encircled Katie's head, one at the back to steady it, the other firmly upon her forehead. The one on her forehead felt nice and cool. "Honey, you're burnin' up!" Birdie snatched her hands back and stared at her, hands on hips. "You got sunstroke, that's what—how you feelin'? Head ache?"

Katie nodded. "Like hell."

"Uh-huh. And dizzy. I see it—your eyes don't look good to me. Here, now—sit down."

"Thirsty," Katie said doggedly, licking her lips.

"Uh-huh . . ." Birdie had turned, and was bustling around the shed with amazing agility, considering her bulk. In another moment a cold, wet towel was pressing against Katie's forehead. Another was draped over the back of her neck. A large plastic drinking glass was placed firmly in her hand, and she was being instructed: "*Drink!*"

She did, shamelessly gulping. When the glass was empty—Katie thought it had probably contained lemonade—she took a deep breath and paused while she evaluated her body's responses, and then reported, "I think I'm going to throw up."

"No, you ain't," Birdie said flatly.

After further consideration Katie decided the cook was probably right; it was only the pounding in her head that made her stomach feel so queasy. All she wanted to do was go lie down somewhere, preferably someplace dark and *quiet.*

Because, for some reason, just to add to her torment, the world had suddenly become very noisy. It was filling up with yips and shouts and masculine laughter, and the unmistakable sound of horses. A great many horses.

"Oh, damn," Birdie said. "There's the men already! Honey, you better get to your tent and lie down."

"Okay," Katie mumbled obligingly; it sounded like a good idea to her. She stood up, and the wet towels landed with a plop on the hard dirt floor. "Where's it?"

"Just over yonder." Katie squinted, trying to see where

Birdie was pointing. Birdie's voice had developed a peculiar echo. "Can you make it, hon? I can't take you myself, I'm gonna have twenty hungry cowboys in here in a minute. Where's that damn Snake? He brought you in, didn't he? *Snake!*"

The cook's bellow ricocheted through Katie's skull. Trying, without much success, to hold her head together, she stumbled toward the doorway. Just before she got there, it suddenly seemed like a very smart thing to do to sit down on the floor.

Two

Cole damn near stepped on her. About the last thing he expected to find when he heard Birdie yell for Snake was a pair of long, slim female legs sprawled across the cookhouse doorway. Swearing, he dropped to one knee beside his biographer.

"I was afraid of this."

"Yeah, well—" Birdie gave the chili pot a hefty stir and then shook the ladle at him. "I'd like to know what that worthless Snake was thinkin' about, lettin' that lady ride all day without no hat! You know she ain't used to it!"

"Yeah, well, don't be too hard on poor old Snake," Cole said dryly, keeping his eyes on Ms. Winslow's greenish complexion. "From what I've seen of this lady, I'd say he probably gave it his best shot." The "lady" opened her mouth and made a sound of protest, which he ignored. "Come help me get her up off the floor, will you?"

Birdie gave a robust titter. "You mean to tell me

Mister Macho himself can't pick up one little bitty skinny woman? Shame on you—you gettin' soft."

Cole grinned. "They don't pay me for my muscles."

Birdie's snort shook her whole body. "Well, I hope to goodness you don't get paid for brains—bringing that poor thing all the way up here, and by horseback! I bet you a dollar she'd never been on a horse in her life before today. Tomorrow she ain't even gonna be able to walk!"

Ms. Winslow croaked, "I'm . . . *fine!*"

"Sure you are," Cole muttered, frowning into wide, unfocused eyes.

"Huh," Birdie said. "She ain't either—she's got sunstroke, that's what."

"Yeah . . ." With a sigh Cole got to his feet and hoisted Ms. Winslow up beside him. Her knees buckled. He grabbed her around the waist before she could sink back down to the floor, and as he did so the clip that held her hair together came loose, spilling it across his face and shoulder. As he was spitting the auburn mass out of his mouth he noticed that it was very soft, and smelled like . . . apples.

"Now," Birdie was saying, "you take some liniment and alcohol and see that she gets rubbed down good— *Cole Grayson!* What do you think you're doing?"

Cole was bending over, in the process of inserting his shoulder under Ms. Winslow's midsection. "What does it look like?" He grunted, straightening up and shifting his burden so that it was more balanced. It gave a squeak of outrage, which he chose to ignore. "She can't walk, and I'm taking her to her tent."

"Not like that, you ain't!" Birdie turned from giving the chili pot another stir and fixed him with a black glare. "That ain't no way to carry a lady!"

"Look—it's the most efficient way to carry a human body—ask any fireman. Besides which it gives me a hand free to carry the liniment. Where is it?"

Birdie pointed with the ladle to the medicine chest

under the dry sink. "Right there, where it's always been. But you can just come back for it." She planted herself between Cole and the door and folded her arms over her bosom. It was an imposing sight. "Cole, you ain't takin' that poor lady out through the men with her bottom stickin' up in the air. You embarrass her like that, and I guarantee she'll never forgive you for it!"

"Hmm." Cole stared thoughtfully at the neat, denim-clad bottom draped over his shoulder. It was a very nice bottom, come to think of it, considering how slender she was. He had a feeling Birdie was right. He also had a feeling that it was something he might come to regret . . . very much.

She was being awfully quiet—not struggling or protesting at all, but only quivering a little—and that worried him. When he shifted her from his shoulder to his arms, she stirred and drew a breath that was more like a muted sniffle. He looked down at her in surprise. Her eyes were closed, but he distinctly saw the glitter of teardrops under her lashes. For a long time he just stared at them, ignoring Birdie's snort of approval and mutters of sympathy. He was getting a funny feeling in his chest, and that *really* surprised him. He wasn't usually susceptible to women's tears—he'd seen the waterworks turned on and off on command too many times.

Lifting one eyebrow at Birdie and bracing himself for the good-natured razzing of the cowboys, he carried his biographer outside into the chill Sierra dusk.

He'd had her tent set up some distance from the main camp, in a nice little stand of pines, so she'd have some privacy. It was a pretty good walk, carrying a hundred and twenty or so pounds of limp female. And to make it more difficult, he had to stop halfway there to let the remuda go by. It was a little like waiting at the crossing for a freight train. As he stood there watching the herd of working horses make their nightly dash for the freedom, grass, and cool water in the meadow, K. T. Winslow finally stirred and opened her eyes.

She lifted her head and muttered, "What is that—an earthquake?"

Cole grunted. "Nope. Stampede."

"Oh." Her eyes slowly focused on his face . . . widened . . . and then closed. "Oh, Lord! I don't believe this."

"What's the matter?"

"This is ridiculous."

"Yeah, I know. Don't say I didn't warn you. Would you mind putting your head back down on my shoulder? It makes it a little easier to carry you."

The last of the horses had gone thundering by, leaving a thick cloud of dust.

Ms. Winslow murmured, "You don't have to carry me. I'm fine." But she had already tucked her head into the curve of his neck and shoulder. Now she gave a sigh and put her hands around his neck. Somehow, that brought her upper body up close against his chest. As he hefted her weight, adjusting his grip on her for the rest of the trek to her tent, Cole was thinking about how well they fit. Amazing, too, how good she felt—thighs firm in his hand, breasts nice soft pillows against his chest, hair a silky tickle under his jaw . . .

Monitoring his body's responses with a mixture of amusement and astonishment, Cole thought that he was either as badly out of shape as Birdie had suggested, or it was going to be one very interesting summer.

She didn't stir again until he went to lower her to the sleeping bag in her tent. Without taking her arms from around his neck she opened her eyes and regarded him with solemn accusation. "You realize," she muttered, licking her lips, "that this is a terrible cliché."

"Yeah?"

She nodded, winced, and closed her eyes again. Her voice was slurred. "Yeah. I'd never get away with writing a scene like this."

Cole gently disengaged her arms. "Is that a fact? Well, you're not dealing with fiction now, you know. I'm afraid life's full of clichés, darlin'."

She settled into the air mattress with a little wiggle and gave a husky laugh. "Wanna hear another one?"

"Sure." Cole paused in the tent opening to look down at her. She was lying on her side, with one flushed cheek pillowed on her hand. In the waning light she looked young and unguarded. Vulnerable.

Her voice was a breathy sigh. "I always fall in love with my heroes."

"Oh, yeah?"

"Yeah. Madly."

Cole laughed softly and headed back to the cookhouse for the liniment and rubbing alcohol.

A very interesting summer . . .

Katie drifted in and out of dreams, dreams that seemed to consist mainly of scenes from old Cole Grayson movies. In every single one Cole was carrying some famous and incredibly gorgeous actress in his arms.

There was the scene from *Without Honor* where Cole picks up Rachel Warner and carries her out of her husband's, the governor's, mansion while she kicks and pounds his broad shoulders with her fists. . . .

And from that classic John Huston movie, *Diablo,* the wonderful scene played in silhouette against the hellish glow of the burning town, where Sophia Romano transforms in Cole's arms from burden to lover . . .

And, of course, the most famous of all—Sara Fielding in *Rio Grande,* spitting fire as Cole carries her out into the middle of the shallow river and dumps her in, flounces and all . . .

Cole Grayson standing in the dust left by a herd of stampeding horses, cradling a languid and semiconscious . . . *Katie Taylor?*

Whoa, Katie thought as the dream did a slow dissolve into reality. What was wrong with that picture? Plain Kate, frowsy, redheaded housewife with crooked teeth and twenty excess pounds, in the arms of a famous movie star? Ridiculous.

She opened her eyes and stared up into a pool of amber light that cast weird shadows on a dark green background. Well, of course she could hardly call herself a housewife these days, the teeth weren't crooked anymore, and she'd never see those twenty pounds again, thank goodness, but that didn't make the picture any less ridiculous. Or humiliating.

The light was merciless. She groaned and closed her eyes as a vortex of pain caught her and spun her in a slowly descending spiral.

"Katherine," said a voice. "Ms. Winslow?"

"Katie." She moaned. "Just plain Katie." And then, as she recognized the voice, she added, "Oh, no."

There was a soft chuckle. "Yep. 'Fraid so."

Katie levered one eye open and glared at the tall, graceful form bending over her. "Do you have any idea how humiliating this is?"

Cole Grayson shrugged. "Yeah, believe it or not, I think I do. But you know, you brought it on yourself. Have you always been so stubborn?" There was real curiosity in his voice.

"I'm supposed to ask those kinds of questions," Katie muttered, and then sighed and lifted an arm to cover her eyes. "Oh, probably. I didn't get where I am by being wishy-washy."

Cole gave a short, dry laugh. Katie heard the clank of glass and felt him kneel beside her air mattress. From under her arm she said in glum accusation, "You did this on purpose, didn't you?"

There was a soft snort. "Ms. Winslow, I don't think I could manage to inflict a case of sunstroke on somebody without her wholehearted cooperation."

"You know what I mean. Your 'condition'—that the interviews be conducted up here, in this place." Katie spoke very carefully, trying not to slur her words. "Mr. Grayson, you were hoping I'd chicken out, weren't you?"

There was a short silence, then the sound of expelled breath. "Yeah, I guess I was."

"Well, that's honest. But why?" Katie lowered her arm and looked up into the face that had graced uncounted theater screens and feminine dreams. If she hadn't felt so rotten the sight would have taken her breath away. "Wouldn't it have been a lot simpler—and more effective—just to say no?"

In the golden light of the kerosene lantern, Cole's eyes were a mellow and warm brown. They made him seem somehow gentler, more human, less like the fierce bird of prey she'd faced this afternoon in the meadow. When, without warning, the eyes suddenly crinkled at the corners, she felt a funny catch in her chest, almost like a hiccup.

"Couldn't," Cole said with a shrug. "I'd already said yes. Given my word."

"And your word is—"

"My bond," Cole said, then laughed, mocking himself. "Right. A matter of personal honor."

"Figures." Katie sighed. "Well, it's not exactly an auspicious beginning for a working relationship, is it?"

"I don't know; it's too soon to tell." Cole settled himself on his knees. The bucket he'd brought with him gave another clink, and Katie hoisted herself on one elbow in an effort to see what was in it. The maneuver proved to be a mistake.

"What is that?" she whispered when the danger of throwing up seemed to have passed.

"Liniment and alcohol. Liniment for your sore muscles, alcohol to bring your fever down. 'Fraid I'm going to have to ask you to take off your shirt."

Katie made a croaking noise that was meant to be a laugh. "You're not serious!" His silence was eloquence itself. "Over my dead body!"

"Oh, I don't really expect it to come to that," Cole

drawled. "But you are one sick lady, and you happen to be my responsibility. I'm no doctor, and I don't even have a thermometer, but your body temperature is way up, and that's dangerous. It has to come down. Now, there's a creek out there in the meadow, full of snowmelt runoff. I *could* pick you up and carry you down there and put you in—"

"Sara Fielding," Katie muttered. "*Rio Grande,* nineteen sixty—"

"But I don't think you'd like it much. The alternative is a nice, soothing alcohol rub. Which is it gonna be?"

Katie groaned. She seemed to be doing a lot of that lately. "Can't somebody else? I mean, for Pete's sake!"

"Honey." Cole's voice had that quiet ring of authority she'd encountered once before. "There are about twenty guys out there who'd love to do this. You say the word—"

"I'll do it myself!"

"Oh, yeah? You can't even lift your head up."

"Birdie," Katie said desperately. "Can't Birdie do it?"

"Birdie's got hungry men to feed," Cole snapped with finality. "Come on, Katherine, quit acting like a simpering maiden. Neither of us is a kid. If it'll help, I'll turn my back while you ditch the shirt and get yourself turned over. Hell, you've probably sunbathed on public beaches in less. I'll give you . . . thirty seconds."

"Count *slowly,*" Katie mumbled, and began, with bitter resignation, to unbutton her shirt. She felt too awful to put up more of a fight. Her fingers were shaking so badly, she thought for one horrible moment she might have to ask for Cole's help with the buttons, but she managed the job with time to spare. "Ready," she said softly, too relieved to be able to lay her throbbing head down to care about the vulnerable expanse of her naked back.

Her *almost*-naked back. There was a brief silence while Cole surveyed the white stripe of her bra; and then without comment, deftly unhooked it and pushed it out of his way. A moment later Katie sucked in air as her spine contracted involuntarily in reaction to the stab of icy liquid. She swore under her breath.

"That's *cold!*"

"That's the idea. Lie still, or you're apt to reveal more than I think you'd care to."

Katie lay stiff as a board; it took every bit of her concentration to keep from flinching every time the cold spread to a new centimeter of skin. So it was several minutes before she lifted her head again and said in a voice like the croaking of a frog, "What—? That smells like *whiskey!*"

"Jack Daniel's," Cole confirmed placidly. "Birdie was out of rubbing alcohol."

"I *hate* whiskey!" Katie wailed weakly, wondering whether she was closer to laughter or tears.

"This is a cow camp. What do you expect? Dom Perignon?" Cole's voice was husky with what Katie could only assume was amusement. Though in the next minute she wasn't sure; his voice deepened and acquired indefinable overtones that made her spine tighten and her skin tingle in ways completely unrelated to either fever or Jack Daniel's. She was all at once terribly aware of the roughness of Cole's hands—and the gentleness.

Cole cleared his throat. "Although . . . hmm. Dom Perignon—you know, that idea has possibilities."

"Don't be funny," Katie managed, faintly.

Cole's answering chuckle seemed to come from deep inside him. His hands had settled into a slow, massaging rhythm; they moved in circles over her back, down her spine as far as her waistband would allow, down the sides of her waist and under, lifting her a little in order to reach her belly, spreading silky coolness over her fevered skin. Slowly, so slowly, they traveled upward over her ribs, just barely—accidentally?—brushing the sides of her breasts before following the line of her underarms outward, all the way to her wrists.

Katie pressed her lips together and tried to breathe

deeply and regularly. It was impossible. She began to shiver.

"Well," Cole said at last, "I think that ought to do it." Katie heard the sounds of the top being put back on the bottle of whiskey, and of the bottle being put back into the bucket. The clink of glass on glass. The sibilance of indrawn breath. "Now for the liniment. Those leg muscles of yours are going to be—"

"No." Katie's voice was no more than a whisper. She closed her eyes and sniffed loudly. There was no longer any doubt which she was closer to, because one tear had managed to squeeze through her tightly shut lids. "No. I'm not letting you rub that stuff on my legs. Don't you understand? You're . . . that's enough. Just . . . *enough!*"

There was silence, filled with tensions Katie wasn't up to figuring out. Then Cole expelled his breath and stood up.

"Yeah . . . I do understand." His voice was very soft; it still carried that odd huskiness. "And I think you're probably right."

Katie heard the bucket's contents clank as he moved away from her.

"Good night, Katherine." There was a barely audible sound as the tent flap dropped into place, and then the sounds of the camp and the Sierra night closed in.

Katie lay still, listening to the noises that had been there all along, though she hadn't been aware of them: the soft roar of wind in the pines, the giddy chorus of frogs, a disappointed whinny from the wrangler's horse, left behind in the corral; a distant reply from the rest of the herd, night-grazing in the meadow. From the cook shed came the strumming of a guitar, and then, as Cole joined the other men, the comforting sound of masculine conversation. A moment later a tenor voice blurred by the accents of the Southwest picked up the chorus of a song Katie had sung when she was young. He was joined first by a few voices, and then, with shouts and laughter, by the rest.

• • •

Katie woke up feeling and smelling as if she'd had a hard night on the town. She reeked of Jack Daniel's. Every muscle in her body felt bruised. Her head still ached, though not with the awful pounding of the day before. There was a gnawing ache in her belly she thought was probably hunger. And never in her entire life had she known a more compelling need for a bathroom. And for a bath.

She sat up, groaning and swearing, and was slightly mollified to find that her luggage had been neatly stashed at the back of the tent. That luggage, trim and elegant in navy blue nylon, had been a present from the twins on the occasion of her first trip to New York, her first appearance on network television. It had seen her through airports and hotels all over the world. Here it looked as out of place as a pair of dusty saddlebags in the front lobby of the Biltmore. She had a sudden weird sense of having stepped into a time warp. Here she was, quintessential woman of the eighties, lost and alone in the Old West—marooned, like the Connecticut Yankee in King Arthur's court.

Well, not exactly marooned, she acknowledged as she searched through a suitcase for clean underwear. The luggage had come in by helicopter. *She* could have come in by helicopter, if she hadn't a stubborn and long-standing policy against flying in anything smaller than a 747. A policy, she decided, that in light of this current fiasco she was going to have to rethink.

It was very quiet. Although a glance at her watch told her it wasn't even nine o'clock yet, the men had probably been gone for hours, including, presumably, the man she'd come so far, and endured such torture and humiliation, to interview.

She heaved a sigh, which collapsed into a groan when she tried to augment it with a stretch. She had to assume Cole Grayson would get around to her sooner or later and in his own good time. She'd already acknowledged that legends must be humored, and last night, unless that had been a dream—she'd had such a lot of dreams!—Cole had told her he meant to honor his commitment to this biography. He'd given his *word*. Katie rolled her eyes skyward. Of course, in the hero's code of behavior that was as good as an iron-clad contract!

Was the man for real? Good question. So far, she had the feeling Cole Grayson could have been acting a part, playing a role from one of his own movies. Perhaps she hadn't even caught a glimpse of the real Cole Grayson yet. She wondered suddenly, with a feeling of futility, whether she ever would; whether, in fact, there was any point to this project. The real Cole Grayson, was probably carefully wrapped and protected by layers and layers of hero's image. It would take some doing to peel them all away, and, considering this horrendous beginning, she wasn't at all sure that she was the one who could do it.

Katie eased her battered body into pink sweats, being especially careful of the raw patches on the insides of her knees. She rolled clean underwear into a bundle with a towel and a pair of new Levi Five-oh-one's, and then stepped into the fresh, pine-scented morning.

A wistful notion struck: perhaps she didn't want to peel away Cole's layers of image. Maybe it would be better to leave the fantasy alone. . . . The idea stuck in her mind, hovering like one of the little white butterflies she saw dancing over the meadow.

Birdie was in the cook shed, pounding on an enormous mound of bread dough with an energy that seemed motivated by animosity. Katie watched in awe for a moment from the safety of the doorway and then moved cautiously forward.

Birdie grunted a greeting without missing a beat in her attack on the dough. "You lookin' better this mornin'. Hungry?"

"Starving," Katie said.

"Well, coffee's on the stove. I put away some ham and potatoes and biscuits. It'll just take me a minute to fry up some eggs." She gave the dough one final punch and seemed to consider it vanquished. Giving it a satisfied slap, she heaved her bulk around to the stove and hefted a huge black enamel coffeepot.

Katie watched in wonder as Birdie poured something that resembled molten lava into a tin mug, then hauled a covered skillet out of the oven. When she took off the lid, Katie gulped, and murmured, "Oh . . . really, I think . . . this will do just fine. Don't bother with the eggs."

"No bother," Birdie snapped. "You need some fattenin' up. You're too damn skinny. With more meat on your bones the saddle won't rub you so raw, know what I mean? Now . . ." She slapped a couple of baking-powder biscuits on top of the two thick slices of ham and the mound of hashed brown potatoes she'd already piled onto an enameled tin plate and plunked it down on one of three long tables that filled the open end of the shed. "You just set down here and get started on this while I fry you some eggs. Like 'em up or over?"

"Over," Katie said faintly, accepting defeat. There was something she needed more urgently than food. "But could I get you to keep this warm a little while longer? What I really would like"—she laughed a bit desperately—"is a bathroom."

"Ain't no *bathroom*. Best we got is the outhouse. It's over by the cabin." Birdie gave Katie a sideways look, full of doubt. "Ain't what you're used to, honey, but it's what we got."

Katie thanked her and went plodding off in the direction the cook had indicated, filled with resignation and rekindled thoughts of vengeance.

Under Birdie's stern and watchful eye Katie did her best with breakfast, but after disposing of barely half the food on her plate she had to concede defeat. Birdie grumbled, and seemed to take it so much to heart that, to distract and pacify her, Katie asked about bathing facilities, even though she was pretty sure, after her visit to the outhouse, what the answer was going to be.

"Huh," Birdie said, confirming her guess and her fears. "Honey, the only 'facilities' we got around here is the creek or a bucket. I can give you a bucket of nice warm water and a bar of soap and a washrag, and you can take it to your tent. That's what I do. Now, the boys, they like to jump in that creek, but then, I always *did* say a man had to be *crazy* to be a *cowboy.*" Birdie had renewed her assault on the bread dough, apparently having decided its docility wasn't to be trusted.

Katie sighed. It was inevitable, she supposed. She should have just let Cole dump her in the creek the night before and been done with it. At least she wouldn't have been smelling like a skid-row bum this morning. And that smell was definitely beyond the capabilities of a bucket and rag! Gathering her bundle of clothes into her arms she announced her intention to take a bath in the creek.

The cook's chuckle—more a low titter, actually—shook her whole body. "Honey, I hope you got Eskimo blood in you. That creek's nothin' but melted snow, don't you know that? I'll keep the coffeepot on. You gonna need thawin' out when you get back! And don't stay in too long, either, or somebody'll have to fetch you out with a pair a' tongs!"

Katie threw her a martyred look as she left to make her way in a bowlegged waddle down the slope to the meadow.

It was past midmorning, and the sun had long since burned off the early mists and frosts. There was a shimmering light over everything, and a low murmur of sound; of breezes stirring through grasses, of busy insects and scurrying ground creatures and the constant chatter and chuckle of the creek. As Katie walked, clouds of tiny gnats rose from the grass, and grasshoppers erupted and sailed away with a harsh, rasping noise. The sun began to burn her back and shoulders through the fabric of her shirt. She could feel it burning, too, in the part on the top of her head, and, remembering the disasters that high-altitude sun could bring, hastily piled her bundle of clothing on top of her head to shield it.

From under that shade she scanned the meadow. Nothing but serenity as far as the eye could see. It was beautiful, she had to admit, if you overlooked the abundance of insect life. She could see how all this natural beauty and solitude might renew and revitalize a man buffeted by the pressures and responsibilities of superstardom. Actually, she'd been tempted on occasion to "chuck it all too."

She was completely out of sight of the camp, in a world of her own, a lake of green sheltered by tall pines and canopied by a sky of such intense blue, it seemed opaque. She'd been following the creek, more or less, looking for a good bathing spot, but had found the banks steep, and thick with reeds that seemed capable of hiding things Katie would just as soon not risk stepping on. Here, though, she found a spot that looked like a picture-book swimming hole—a wide place with sloping, grassy banks. And the water was so clear, she could see the grass growing in the pale, sandy bottom, a feature she found reassuring. Tiny minnows nibbled at the algae that grew in the warm shallows.

With a sigh that was a little less put-upon than previous ones, she dropped her bundle on the grass and sat down to take off her shoes. With one final furtive glance around, she stood up and pulled off her sweats. It was an interesting feeling, standing naked in a meadow under a wide blue sky, with the hot sun and silky breezes caressing her body. She was beginning to smile as she tiptoed gingerly into the water.

The shriek that erupted from her was involuntary,

forced from her by the shock of pure ice water. But she'd grown up within walking distance of the Pacific Ocean, and knew the futility of postponing the inevitable. She held her breath for a quick one-two-three count and then plunged, gasping, into deeper water. Numbed but exhilarated, she rubbed at her skin until it was pink and tingling, ridding herself of trail dust and sweat, the stink of horses and Jack Daniel's. By the time she'd begun to rinse out her long, heavy hair, her body had become accustomed enough to the cold that she could actually relax in the water and let the current flow through her hair, spreading it out from her head in a dark, rippling fan. . . .The water moved over her naked body with icy fingers that raised gooseflesh, shivered her breasts into painful tautness, pulled her muscles into knots, and set every nerve to tingling. . . .

At first Katie didn't separate the new rhythmic sound from the other meadow music. By the time the primitive sentry in her brain had begun to shriek, "*Horse!*" it was too late. All she could do was make for the cattails at the downstream end of the pool, shrink into their meager shadows, and hope the rider would go on by without noticing her.

A faint hope, considering she'd left her pink sweats sprawled on the bank.

The sound of hooves slowed . . . and stopped. Katie heard the creak of saddle leather as the rider dismounted, the jingle of a bridle as the reins were dropped. Footsteps . . . or rather, the swish of cowboy boots through meadow grass. With fatalistic dread, Katie peered through the reeds. And groaned aloud.

"Ms. Winslow?" Cole Grayson's voice held wonder . . . and amusement. "*Katherine?*"

"What?" Katie snapped. Her jaws were already beginning to quiver.

Cole noticed. "Katherine, don't you think you ought to come out of there before you freeze your . . . self?" He had hurriedly edited himself; he was obviously about one syllable away from laughter.

"I can't," Katie said grimly. She was having to hug herself tightly in order to talk, as her whole body was quaking.

"Ah. I see."

"I hope not," Katie said fervently, adding, "I've seen this too. *Man From Nowhere,* right? With . . . Julie whatshername." With wonderful disregard for reason she blurted out, *"Did you plan this?"*

Cole's laughter rang out like a bell. "I've got a pretty fair imagination, but I'd have had to stretch it some to put you in that creek, especially after yesterday . . . and last night!"

"After last night you didn't think I'd want a *bath?"*

"Well, yeah," Cole said, still laughing, "but not in ice water."

Her lofty disdain somewhat hampered by chattering teeth, Katie retorted, "Ha! I grew up in Oxnard—"

"Oxnard!"

"—swimming in the Pacific Ocean in all seasons. This creek is—"

"I know what that creek is. And I wouldn't stay in there too long if I were you."

"I didn't intend to stay in *this* long!" Katie shouted, not far from anger and a lot closer to tears than she cared to be, both from mortification and from a growing ache in her nether regions. "If you have even the tiniest shred of decency—"

"Well," Cole drawled, "I think I've probably got about that much." Katie was beginning to notice that he had a tendency to lapse into that Texas drawl now and then; right now she found it absolutely infuriating. She sniffled, and held her breath while she listened to the sounds of his leaving.

"Adiós, Katherine." He spoke softly to his horse, and the muffled thud of hoofbeats on turf began to retreat.

Katie let go of her breath in a jerky gust of relief and started to wade out of the numbing water. A moment later she was doubled over, feeling as if someone had whacked her with a club. Pain seemed to be everywhere—in her calves, her thighs, arches, buttocks—every muscle in her body was tied in knots of iron. She couldn't move. Panic tore through her. She knew she was in real trouble, and that her only hope of rescue was riding off into the heat-shimmer on his big black horse.

All her hard-won feminine pride and independence went downstream. In the very best damsel-in-distress tradition, Katherine Taylor Winslow opened up her mouth and screamed, *"Help!"*

Three

Cole loomed above her, leaning with studied uncon-
cern on the pommel of his saddle. The hat he'd given
her the day before rode low on his forehead, shading
his eyes. He thumbed it back and shook his head.

"Lady, you are in one hell of a pickle."

"Cramps," Katie said wheezing. "In my legs. Can't
. . . walk."

"Figures." Cole grunted and dismounted. "Do you
realize I haven't seen you ambulatory yet?" With real
curiosity he asked, "Have you always been this good at
gettin' yourself into embarrassing situations?"

If she hadn't already been shaking with cold and
blind with pain, she'd probably have become both now—
from rage. "There you go again. I'm supposed . . . to
ask . . . the questions, dammit!"

Cole shrugged. "Fine with me. Fire away." He disappeared from view. Katie altered her own position among
the reeds enough to observe that he'd sat down on the
bank and was taking off his boots.

"What—what are you doing?"

"Taking off my boots."

"I can *see* that. What for?"

Cole's grin was wicked, a real heart-stopper. Katie wondered if she was ever going to feel well enough in his presence to appreciate its full effect. "I don't think I care to ruin a good pair of broken-in boots, darlin', not even for a pretty woman."

Katie's heart did stop. She could have sworn it did. "You're not . . . coming in here . . . after me?" Her voice disappeared in an incredulous squeak.

"Well, now, what did you think I was going to do when you hollered for help?" Cole's tone was matter-of-fact, but edging toward exasperation. "You've got to get out of that water, and damn quick, and you can't move. Seems to me we've got no choice here."

"But I . . . you can't . . ." Katie took a deep breath and blurted out, "Okay, then, but close your eyes!"

"Hell's bells, woman, I've seen—"

"I don't care what you've seen. You haven't seen *me*. Close your eyes!"

Cole exploded. "Look, I'm not crazy about the idea of getting in that water with my clothes on, even if it *is* to keep a crazy lady from dying of hypothermia, and if you think—"

"I don't care," Katie said on a sob—histrionics, it seemed, were contagious. "If I do die of hypothermia in here it will be on your conscience!"

There was silence, then a sigh and a splash, followed by a gasp and a muffled, "*Damn*, that's cold!"

"*Cole?*"

"Look, they're closed, dammit—scout's honor. Now, shut up. No, on second thought I guess you'd better keep talking so I can find you."

A moment later Katie was treated to the sight of America's number-one male box-office attraction wading toward her through the reeds, in ice water up to his waist. Except for his boots he was fully clothed, even to his hat. His eyes were squeezed shut, and his teeth were tightly clenched, though that didn't do much to stem a steady stream of muttered curses.

Katie stretched out a bluish hand to touch his arm. In a small, chastened voice she said, "Here I am."

Cole merely nodded, set his jaw in grim lines, and placed his hand with suspicious accuracy on the nape of her neck. With her coordinates thus established he leaned over, hooked his other arm around her crabbed knees and hoisted her, nude and dripping, into his arms.

Katie swallowed a gasp and a comment in one gulp. A glance up at Cole's face told her he was awfully close to smashing his public image all to smithereens. He'd even stopped swearing; somehow the silence seemed much more ominous.

She could have sworn the trip back to the bank took several hours. Cole had to feel for each step, testing the creek's treacherous, sandy bottom, and Katie wasn't in any shape this time to make his job easier. At one point, teetering momentarily off-balance, Cole snapped at her, "Dammit, I'm gonna drop you if you don't loosen up. And stop shivering."

"I can't." Katie sniffed, wretched and contrite. "I'm sorry."

She saw Cole's jaw tighten and felt his chest expand. His eyelids quivered, but he didn't say anything. A moment later she felt her numbed feet being lowered, with unanticipated gentleness, to the ground. Cole's hand steadied her as she tried to stand.

"If I can just . . . I need to reach my towel." Her voice was so jerky that it was hard to make her words intelligible.

Cole just nodded, and murmured, "Where is it?"

"There . . . a little to your right—that's it."

Keeping a firm grip on her arm with one hand, Cole stretched, groped, and found the towel with the other. His face was absolutely impassive as he spread it out and held it wide. After peering up into the shadow under his hat brim to assure herself that his eyes really were closed, Katie turned stiffly into it.

The ends of the towel came around her body, along with Cole's arms. He pulled her back against him and wrapped the towel—and his arms—firmly across her front.

This time Katie failed to restrain either gasp or comment. "What—what are you doing?"

Cole's chest made a sound like a volcano. His breath rumbled against her back and erupted in a furious gust above her head. "Dammit, what do you *think* I'm doing? I never saw anybody like you! I'm trying my best to warm your bones, that's what I'm doing! Woman, I know I've been up here a long time, but I think I'd still like my women at least *warm*—and *willing!*"

With a disgusted snort he dropped his arms and stalked up the bank, walking bowlegged and grumbling bitterly under his breath about redheaded women and wet Levis.

Katie watched him for a minute in silence. Then, knowing the situation was far beyond salvaging, she pushed lank strands of wet hair out of her face, and tried to sit down.

Her agonized wail stopped Cole in his tracks. Katie saw him freeze, shift his shoulders, and tuck his thumbs through his belt loops. Miserably she watched him turn, swearing with eloquence, and stomp back to where she was crouched, clutching her towel, unable to move either up or down. Given the vehemence of his vocabulary, his hands were a surprise—they eased her gently down onto the grassy bank, almost as if she were a very small child.

Moving gingerly in his wet pants, he settled himself at her feet. "Bet you didn't use that liniment I gave you, did you? If you'd let me rub you down last night you wouldn't be in this mess." He glanced up at her, and for one moment there was silence, while his eyes seemed to glow. Katie wondered if he was remembering that odd tension between them over that particular issue. . . . Then he seemed to collect himself, and looked back down at her legs. "Or, if you'd at least done it yourself—let me see here . . . good night, woman!" He leaned his arm across one knee and gave her his eagle's glare. "Why in the hell didn't you tell me about those saddle sores?"

"Because," Katie quavered, trying to hold her spine straight; she was wracked with shivers. "I didn't know they were saddle sores, dammit! And would you stop calling me that!"

"What?" Cole looked confused.

"Woman," Katie said, breathing heavily through her nose.

"Ah." Cole's smile was ominously benign. "And what would you like me to call you?"

Katie stared at him for a frigid moment or two and then said, "Ms. Winslow will do nicely."

"All right with me . . . *Ms. Winslow,*" Cole muttered, clenching his teeth. "Sit still and let me see what I can do with your latest disaster."

Since she had very little choice in the matter, Katie leaned back on her hands and closed her eyes. She was angrier and more frustrated than she could remember being in years. Incredible—here she was in just the sort of position she'd promised herself she'd never find herself in again, helpless, and dependent on a man. Even in the worst days of her marriage she'd never felt so childish and ridiculous. Where was her hard-won self-assurance now? Where was her self-esteem? She'd always had a certain inherent dignity, at least, but even that seemed to have abandoned her!

Cole's hand closed around her ankle. Her breath hissed through her teeth as he lifted it carefully into his lap.

"I think," he murmured, drawling again, "that this is where I'm supposed to say, 'You know you're beautiful when you're angry?' "

Katie sniffed. "Boy, have you got the wrong script."

Infuriatingly, he just laughed—his temper seemed to

be as short-lived as it was short-fused. Now he appeared completely at ease, and totally engrossed in what he was doing. And what he was doing was making it well-nigh impossible for Katie to prolong her own fit of temper.

He was massaging her foot—stretching and manipulating the cramped arch, rotating the ankle, rubbing and chafing the chilled flesh to bring back warmth and circulation. Nothing had ever felt so good.

Katie slowly and cautiously drew breath and clamped her teeth down hard on her lower lip. She found herself gazing, entranced, at the back of Cole's neck. In spite of the hat and bandana he always wore, it looked sunburned, and as if it would be warm and smooth to the touch.

Just then Cole's probing fingers, following her Achilles tendon upward, found a charley horse in her calf muscle. She jerked and sucked in air. He glanced up at her, one eye shut against the glare of the empty sky.

"Hurt?"

Katie nodded. It did hurt, but that wasn't why she was suddenly incapable of speech.

"Sorry," Cole said softly, and shrugged. "Can't be helped."

Katie could only manage another nod. Now it was his hands that fascinated her—his incredible hands, big, hard, callused by rawhide and hemp, but deft as a surgeon's and gentle as a lover's, magically untying the knots in her muscles.

She'd stopped shivering; the sun was warm across her back and her legs lay relaxed across Cole's lap. The cramps were gone now, and his hands were stroking more than massaging.

Katie cleared her throat and spoke to the back of his head. "You don't think much of me, do you?"

Cole's hands stopped moving but stayed where they were, one just above her knee, the other just below it. He turned his head to look up at her and grinned. "As what? As a cowpoke? Sweetheart, you probably aren't the worst I ever saw, but close to it. As a writer? I've read some of your stuff, and I'd say you're a pretty fair writer. Better than that, or I'd never have said yes to this deal in the first place. Now, as a person . . ." He cocked his head and considered, creases at the corners of his eyes deepening. Katie waited, wondering why she cared so much about the verdict. "As a person, I don't believe I know you well enough yet to know what I think. And as a woman—" The grin turned wicked. "Well, hell, woman, how can I tell, if you keep makin' me close my eyes?"

There was a moment of tense silence, and then Katie burst out laughing. Cole Grayson would never know how close she'd just come to planting a newly operational foot squarely in his ribs and shoving him, hat and all, back into the creek! The impulse was still echoing and rebounding through her nerves; her muscles tingled and quivered with it. She wasn't sure what had stopped her—at some point between impulse and action a tiny voice in her brain had screeched, "That's *Cole Grayson*, you idiot!"

If he'd been any other man . . .

It occurred to Katie later that for such a wild and impossible impulse to have come to her at all, she had to have forgotten, just for that instant, at least, that he *was* Cole Grayson. Lulled by the Sierra sunshine, mesmerized by a pair of magical hands and a sunburned neck, she'd seen him not as a legend, a superstar, but as a man. Arrogant and infuriating, certainly, and very, very attractive, but just a man.

But that was later. Right then all she felt was a sudden jarring awareness that she was wearing a *towel*. Oddly, that revelation seemed to strike her at about the same time it came to Cole that he was sitting there with a lapful of K. T. Winslow's long, naked legs.

The atmosphere became electric, all but crackling with constraint. Katie stiffened and sat up straight, tensing her legs to shift them off of Cole's lap. At the same instant Cole's hands tightened on her legs and lifted them up and away from him. Katie clutched her towel and became very busy tightening it around her. Cole took off his hat, then put it back on. Katie stared down at her toes and wiggled them experimentally.

Cole got to his feet and stood holding out his hand. "Come on. I'll help you up." For some reason, his voice had grown harsh.

It was Katie's turn to squint into the glare. "No, thanks, I think I'll stay here a little longer—"

"I'd have thought you'd had enough sun to last you a while. Come on, I'd like to make sure you really can walk this time. Give me your hand."

Recognizing that ring of implacability in his voice, Katie put her hand in his. She was pretty much resigned to the fact that it wasn't going to be possible to get to her feet with grace and dignity wearing nothing but a towel, not if she wanted to preserve her modesty. And given the choice between dignity and modesty, there was really no contest.

"Okay?" Cole asked when she was vertical and he was holding her by the elbows while she tested her legs. Satisfied that they were indeed functioning, he released her and stepped back. "Well, then. I'll be on my way." He grinned, a familiar flash of wry and rueful charm. "My crew's gonna wonder where in the hell I got to. I just came back for some penicillin. Got a steer with an abscess—foxtail, probably." He hauled himself into his saddle, grimacing at the discomfort of wet denim, and touched the brim of his hat with a forefinger. "See you later."

It was premium-quality, one-hundred-percent pure Cole Grayson.

"Wait!" Katie cried, like someone waking from a trance. It wasn't easy to transform herself into K. T. Winslow while standing in meadow grass, wearing nothing but a towel, her hair drying rampant on her shoulders, but she gave it her best. "You seem to be very busy right now—do you mind if I ask when you expect to have time to spare for me? For the book, I mean," she amended, as a little smile flicked across Cole's face.

For a long moment he just looked down at her from his favorite vantage point, leaning on the pommel of his saddle. Then he lifted his head and looked out over the meadow. His eyes were hidden in the shadow of his hat, and his voice was so soft, it seemed a part of the meadow noise.

"Ah . . . Katherine. Don't you even know you're standing in the middle of one of the most beautiful places on God's green earth? What you need to do is loosen up a little bit—relax and take time to enjoy it. What's the hurry? They got you on a tight deadline?"

Katie shook her head. "No, but—"

"Well, then. Ease up. Relax. Take plenty of time for what's important." He made a clicking sound to his horse, and brought his gaze back to Katie. She could see his eyes now. To her surprise they seemed almost sad. "What you need to do, Ms. Winslow, is make sure you *know* what the important things are."

A moment later he was riding off, while Katie stood alone, frowning.

She wasn't positive, but she thought she might have just been given her first glimpse of the real person inside Cole Grayson.

It was a long time before she moved again. And when she did, she found that she was filled with a vague and giddy excitement. Her mind was restive, like a high-strung thoroughbred at the starting gate; her body was humming like a dynamo, full of energy and vitality. Those were all symptoms she recognized, and the recognition brought its own exhilaration. It was that old creative surge she always got when a new idea really took hold in her.

For better or worse, the Cole Grayson story had her hooked.

• • •

"Where's the lady?" Snake asked Cole that evening in the cook shed over blood-rare steaks and four-alarm chili.

Cole shrugged. "In her tent, I guess."

"Still got sunstroke?"

"Naw—she's fine." Cole was silent for a moment, considering the absence of Ms. Winslow. "I think maybe she's a little bit shy about being the only woman besides Birdie."

"Umm." Snake chewed on the idea along with a chunk of beef. "Lotta women would like that," he observed after a while.

"Yeah." Cole pushed his plate aside and reached for his coffee mug. "She isn't exactly like a lot of women."

"She sure ain't." Snake grunted, mopping up chili with half a biscuit and popping the whole thing into his mouth.

Cole glanced at him but didn't say anything. When Snake was capable of speech again he elaborated.

"You know she never said word one of complaint, comin' up here? Not word one. And she had to be wore out—and hurtin'."

"She's got saddle sores," Cole muttered, shifting on the bench.

"Yeah?" Snake considered this new information thoughtfully. "Well, she never said word one. Most women woulda bitched and whined every step of the way, know what I mean?" It was Snake's turn to push away his empty plate and pick up his mug. Hunched over it, he leaned toward Cole and lowered his voice. "Hey, Cole. You thought about what she's gonna do for . . . you know."

Cole gazed sourly at him and waited for him to come up with a word, though he knew perfectly well what he meant.

Snake coughed, and muttered, "The . . . amenities."

"Amenities?" Cole was torn between guilt and laughter. Snake's vocabulary had some surprises in it.

Snake hitched closer. "Cole, that outhouse ain't fit

for a lady. Least you coulda done is brought in one of them porta-potties. The chopper coulda done it. And what about bathin'? You really expect a nice, classy woman like that to go jump in the *creek*?"

Cole's coffee went down the wrong way. Between coughing spasms he glared so balefully at Snake that Snake got up and went to join the men out by the fire. Billy Claude had his guitar out, anyway, and was starting in on "Bobby McGee," so no doubt Snake wanted to go get his harmonica and join in. Snake probably played the worst harmonica Cole had ever heard, but nobody else seemed to mind.

He wasn't sure which he got tired of listening to first, the music or his conscience, but after a few minutes he swore under his breath and picked up both his and Snake's dishes and went looking for Birdie.

Birdie was peeling potatoes to boil for the next morning's hashbrowns. She looked up when Cole came in, and greeted him with a snort. He dumped the steak bones into the scrap bucket for the dogs and dropped the plates into the washtub.

"Birdie," he said, scowling, "where's that bear grease you give us for saddle sores?"

"Right there, where it's always been," Birdie said, pointing with the potato peeler. "Who needs it?"

"Ms. Winslow," Cole muttered.

"Huh. I thought so. No wonder. Poor thing's got no padding at all."

Cole didn't comment. He had reason to know that wasn't true. He'd thought she was too skinny, too, at first, but he was changing his mind about that—the lady wasn't as scrawny as she looked. In fact—he paused, thoughtfully hefting the can of ointment in his hand— there were darn few people, male or female, who looked better out of their clothes than in them, but K. T. Winslow was one of them.

"She eat tonight?" he asked Birdie.

"Not enough so's you'd notice. Tell you what, since you're goin' that way anyway, why don't you take her a

KATIE'S HERO • 45

dish of that peach cobbler? That woman needs some meat on her. Here, let me put some cream on it."

Cole was a little surprised to hear Springsteen coming from her tent—he'd have guessed classical music, or at least something more mellow, like Neil Diamond. Every woman he knew who was over thirty liked Neil Diamond.

He was so taken up with her musical tastes, he forgot to knock, or do whatever passes for a knock on a tent flap. He just lifted the flap with the hand that had the bear grease in it and ducked inside.

She was sitting cross-legged in the middle of her sleeping bag with the legs of her sweats pushed up as far as they'd go, and was dabbing some kind of antiseptic on her sores with a tissue. She'd taken all that hair of hers and knotted it on top of her head in a haphazard way that left curly strands of it trailing down her neck and across her face. In the light of the overhead lantern her face looked almost gaunt. Yet there was something about the angularity of her cheekbones and jawline, her neck and shoulder, her collarbones, that he was beginning to find very attractive. . . .

"Sorry," he said when she just stared at him without saying anything. "Guess I should have yelled or something. I just brought some stuff for those sores. What you're using won't help much."

She shifted her gaze to the containers in his hands and said, "Which one's for the sores?"

He glanced down at the cobbler and grinned. "Both, actually. Here, this one's to be taken internally." At her look he shrugged. "Birdie's convinced putting some meat on your bones'll prevent saddle sores. She could be right. Cowboys get saddle sores, and most cowboys I know are skinny, so there could be a connection there somewhere." He squatted on his heels beside her and handed her the bowl of cobbler. She took it, poked it with her finger, and put the finger in her mouth.

"Mmm," she said, closing her eyes. "Well, I'm a firm believer in that well-worn saw, 'You can't be too thin or too rich.' "

"Yeah? Well, Birdie'll do her best to fatten you up, I can guarantee it."

"I'm used to it. If you think she's bad, you ought to hear my mother."

Cole chuckled, and was quiet for a few minutes, watching her eat. He'd done what he'd come for; he knew he really ought to be going. "Hey, you know, I really am sorry about . . ." He gestured with the can of bear grease. "Yesterday . . . today. Everything. I should have made better arrangements for . . . the amenities."

She looked directly at him and shrugged. A little smile softened her lips, and when she paused to lick peach juice from them, he realized he was thinking about what it might taste like—her mouth, not the cobbler.

"No problem," she said. "Another motto of mine is, 'Don't sweat the small stuff.' At my age, I hope I've learned not to let a few little inconveniences bother me."

"At your age?" Cole grinned and jerked his head toward the portable tape player on the ground beside her air mattress. "Can't be all *that* old."

She reached out and punched a button, silencing Bruce in mid-wail. "I have eclectic tastes. I got hooked on Bruce when my kids were in high school. Hearing the music brings those years back to me, so I play it when I find myself feeling . . ."

"Lonely?" he prompted.

She gave him another look. "Missing my children. I'm never lonely." Her chin came up a notch, but Cole noticed that she looked down at her bowl just then so he couldn't see her eyes.

"Your kids," he said softly. "They away at school?"

She nodded. "Chris is in premed at Columbia, and Kelly is at West Point."

Cole looked at her for a minute and then asked, "Boys or girls?"

She laughed out loud, which pleased him more than he'd have thought possible. "We all make mistakes. I've learned a lot about naming people since the twins were born. All I can say is, it seemed like a good idea at the time. One of each, actually."

"And now I'm supposed to guess which is which, I suppose."

She leaned back on her hands and studied him with laughter in her eyes. "Can you?"

Cole grinned. "Since you put it like that, it can only be the unexpected . . . right?"

She laughed again; he decided her laugh was another thing he liked about her. "Right. Chris is short for Christopher. My daughter, Kelly, is the West Point cadet."

Cole nodded and muttered, "Figures." And then added softly, "They're a long way from home."

She shrugged again. He noticed she'd lowered her eyes once more, too, gazing at her feet as if she found them fascinating. In a way they were. She was wearing white socks. Cole didn't think he could ever remember seeing a grown woman wearing white socks.

"Their father is stationed in Washington. They wanted to be near him. You see, we were divorced when the twins were just starting high school. They were with me in California while they were in high school, so when they graduated, they wanted a chance to . . . get reacquainted."

"Makes sense," Cole said. "Can I ask you a question?"

A smile pulled at the corners of her mouth. "Just one?"

"That's kind of my point. Why aren't you hollering, 'That's my line!'? Yesterday—"

"Yesterday," she said flatly, "I was being very stupid. And today, if it's possible, even stupider."

"*Stupider?*"

"Hush, it is a word, you know, and even if it weren't

I'm a novelist. I can invent words if I need to. And that's my point. Mr. Grayson—"

"Cole. Please."

"Cole. What I'm trying to do is apologize."

"Apologize?"

"Yeah. And I think that what I'd really like is another chance."

"Another chance?" He was beginning to feel like an idiot, repeating everything she said, but he didn't have the faintest idea what she was talking about.

"Yes." She took a deep breath and held out her hand. "Mr. Grayson—Cole—can we start all over again? Just introduce ourselves and forget yesterday and today ever happened?"

Cole wasn't about to do that, even if it were possible, but he could see that it was important to her, so he took her hand. It felt cold, so he held on to it. It was funny, but he had an urge to tuck it somewhere against his body and keep it there until it grew nice and warm. . . .

"You see," she was explaining, "I was so excited about this project that I sort of forgot who I am. *What* I am. I'm not a journalist or a biographer. I can't just come in and ask a lot of questions and jot down the facts— names, dates, events. I'm a novelist. What I'd forgotten is that I have to get to know my characters pretty well before I write about them. That means that I have to get to know *you*. And"—she took another one of those big breaths—"getting to know someone is a two-way street. I can't expect you to trust me enough to open up to me unless you know me, right?"

Now she looked at him, point blank, but he could see it was hard for her. He had an idea she'd been silently practicing that speech for quite a while. "So," she said, and he could see her brace herself, "fire away."

There were all kinds of things he wanted to know about her, and there would be a time for finding them out . . . little by little. He wasn't in any hurry. So he settled himself beside her and asked casually as he took the lid off the bear grease, "Why didn't you tell anybody about those sores?"

She flinched, though he hadn't touched her yet. Cole had an idea it was because he'd surprised her; she'd expected him to ask something really personal—about her divorce, for starters. What she didn't know was that her answer to his question was going to tell him a lot more about her than the one she'd probably been rehearsing some nice pat answer to.

"Pride," she said, looking rueful. "Ignorance, stupidity. Do cowboys really get saddle sores? Somehow I thought only greenhorns did."

"We all get 'em at one time or another—why do you think Birdie keeps this stuff handy? New saddle, different horse, new pair of Levis . . . lots of different things can cause 'em."

"Really? Oh—" She sucked in her breath as he lifted her leg onto his lap. When he bent her knee and turned it out so he could see the raw patch on the inside, she made a low murmuring noise of protest, which he ignored. He glanced at her and saw that her eyes were closed and her teeth were clamped down on her lower lip. There was the faintest sheen of sweat on her face; in the lantern light it looked like gold dust.

"Yeah," he said. "Really. Only cowboys, often as not, get 'em someplace else. You don't—?"

He was ready with a grin when she opened her eyes to glare at him.

"*No!* I don't." Cole just shrugged and went on dabbing Birdie's concoction on her sores. After a minute she started to smile. "Sorry to disappoint you. I guess that must be one place I have enough padding."

"I'd say you have," Cole said, deadpan. "Just *barely*, though."

She sat up straight. "Were you *peeking?* You rat, if you—"

Laughing, Cole threw up an arm to deflect the punch she aimed at his shoulder. "What kind of a guy do you think I am? If I had, it wouldn't be very gentlemanly to admit it, now, would it?"

"Do you know," she said, breathing through her nose, "how close I came this afternoon to pushing you in that creek? Now I'm sorry I didn't."

"Just out of curiosity, why didn't you?"

She looked a little startled. "Well . . ."

"Yes?"

"Well, I mean, you're—"

"Cole Grayson?"

"Uh, yes."

She was squirming a little, and looking down at her leg and at his hands. It had been a long time since he'd seen a forty-year-old woman blush.

"You know, Katherine," he said softly, "that's something you're going to have to forget, if you're going to write about me with any kind of objectivity."

"I never promised to be objective." Her voice sounded choked. "But you're right. I'm just not sure I can forget it."

"Well," Cole said, shifting himself so he could reach her other leg, "we've been talking here for . . . what, about half an hour? You mean to tell me in all that time you never once forgot you were talking to Cole Grayson?"

"Well . . ."

"Come on, now. You punched me in the shoulder!"

She licked her lips and leveled her gaze at him again. "I guess maybe I did."

Cole wondered, suddenly, why gray was considered a cool color. Contact with those eyes of hers was raising the temperature in the tent by measurable degrees. He drawled, "There, you see? It's not so hard."

She blinked like someone coming out of a trance. "Why do you do that?"

It was his turn to blink. "Do what?"

"Drawl like that. It comes and goes. Why?"

She had him there. She'd surprised him again, and since he didn't have a good comeback he just sat with his hands resting on her leg, looking at her. After a moment of that she dropped her eyes.

"There," he said, quietly triumphant. "Why do you do *that*?"

"What?"

"Look away from me. Hide your eyes."

She opened her mouth and then closed it again. Looked at him and then away. And then gave a funny little laugh and said, "I don't know."

"You see," Cole said softly. "We all have our little shields and defenses, don't we?"

Four

He knew he could have kissed her then, and more than that, if he chose. He wasn't sure why he didn't. It certainly wasn't because he didn't want to. There was just something indefinably tawdry about inviting—no, inveigling!—a woman onto his turf, getting her alone and vulnerable, and then seducing her when her defenses were down! Not exactly the stuff legends like his were made of.

And then it occurred to him to wonder if she expected him to kiss her. The possibility had crossed her mind—he could see it in the way she watched *his* mouth, passing her tongue across her own lips, leaving them invitingly glazed.

The tent was suddenly filled with sexual awareness; the air had weight and substance, the silence was space that his heartbeat filled like a drum resounding in an empty cave. He flicked his gaze upward. Her gaze was meeting his, for once, and he thought he saw confusion in her eyes. Even fear. The thought gave him an odd little jolt behind his ribs.

Funny woman, he mused. Damned funny. She hadn't seemed the least bit awed by him before. Well, maybe a little, enough to keep from kicking him into the creek, anyway. But fear? He was conscious, suddenly, of a feeling he identified as disappointment. It surprised him to realize that the last thing he wanted was for this woman to be afraid of him.

His smile was wry as he eased her leg off of his lap. She gave her head a shake and said, "I'm sorry. What did you say?"

"Didn't say a thing." He rose to his feet. "But I've been thinking about this bathing business. There's a little hot springs about fifteen miles from here. There's a store, a few cabins, some bathhouses. It's a nice, easy ride—maybe a couple hours. Like to go tomorrow?"

"Tomorrow?" She looked doubtfully at the sores on her legs, and he could see she wasn't thrilled about the idea of getting back on a horse.

"Those'll be fine by tomorrow," he assured her. "Absolutely guaranteed. Just put some gauze over 'em to keep the stuff off your clothes." When she still didn't seem very enthusiastic he said softly, "Best thing in the world for sore muscles is a soak in a tub of hot sulfur water."

For a few moments the air seemed to grow thicker, and perceptions narrowed. Then she wrinkled her nose and burst into that laughter he was beginning to like so much. "Ugh. And smells great, too. Okay. What time do we leave?"

"Early."

"Early? How early is 'early'?"

Cole just grinned at her and said, " 'Night, Katherine."

She drew in her breath; it had a funny little catch to it, as if it had intercepted a bubble of laughter. " 'Night, Cole."

Outside her tent he paused, listening to the series of clicks as she ejected one cassette from her tape deck and put in another. A moment later he headed on back to the campfire, smiling and whistling softly. "Here's to you, Mrs. Robinson. . . ." It was nice to know she wasn't feeling lonely anymore.

Lonely. Cole stopped where he was and put his hand on the jigsaw bark of a yellow pine, absently pushing on it as if testing its stability. Across the clearing he could just see the squat hulk of the çook shed, the faint glow of the dying fire. The harmonica and guitar were quiet, the cowboys all bedded down in sleeping bags, with boots and rolled-up Levis for pillows. It would be another long day tomorrow, and dawn came early in the Sierras in the summertime.

Dawn would come just as early for him, but he didn't feel like going to sleep. Not yet. Restlessness, a jumpiness, a kind of prickly effervescence he felt wouldn't let him be at ease. He was surprised by the feelings, not because they were unknown to him, but because they had never come to him up here. It was one of the things that until now had only plagued him down there, among the crowds and concrete canyons. It was one of the things that made him run whenever he could, like an escaping prisoner, back to the solitude of the Sierras.

Solitude. Aloneness. *Loneliness.*

He pushed off from the tree and angled his path uphill toward the corrals, moving with assurance in the darkness across terrain more familiar to him than the rooms of his Los Angeles penthouse. Diablo, all but invisible in the night, whickered a welcome as he climbed the high log fence. He sat hunched over on the top rail of the fence. With his hands between his knees, he gazed down at Katherine Winslow's tent.

It occurred to him that *aloneness* and *loneliness* were two different things entirely. Loneliness had damn little to do with who you were with, or how many people you had around you trying their level best to keep you from being lonely. But he'd always known that. Aloneness—solitude—was sustenance to him; it nourished and renewed him. He came to solitude like a hungry man to a banquet table. And now he realized that the hunger he came to assuage was loneliness.

Down below, the light in Kate's tent winked out, leaving the subtle shades of night unflawed. Resentment flared in him. She had brought the loneliness into his solitude. She was so much of that world, the world that tried each time he ventured into it to wrap him in its tentacles and suck the vitality, the very life, out of him—the world of telephones and talk shows, press releases and premieres, the world of the glittering, the noisy, the gaudy, the *empty*. . . . She had that same brittle elegance he'd come to find so tiresome, and that veneer of classiness that was so effective at keeping the world from knowing what, if anything, was underneath.

And yet, there had been loneliness in *her* eyes too. And he was remembering, with a small sense of wonder, the way she had looked standing barefoot in his meadow, in nothing but a towel, strands of that mahogany hair lying damp on her shoulders and the sun pouring over her like warm honey. Remembering those silly white socks, and the depth of her laughter, as if it truly did come from reservoirs of joy somewhere inside her. Remembering, too, that she had socked him in the shoulder, and that he kept experiencing this weird urge to *warm* her. . . .

He uttered a soft "Huh!" of surprise and levered himself off of the corral fence. As he made his way down the slope, he was thinking that the most acute hunger came from being so close to the table, you could see how good the food looked; so close, you could smell the good smells and your mouth started to water, and all your digestive juices to flow—and you weren't allowed to eat so much as a single bite.

The trail to the hot springs wound through virgin forests of fir and pine so dense that only moss and fern grew on the thick, spongy carpet of pine needles and decayed bark. It was peaceful—so peaceful, it gave Katie the willies. The light had a translucent, underwater quality. The foliage was penetrated by fingers of sunlight that made her think of the enchanted forests in Walt Disney movies. And the silence wasn't really silence at all, but was full of rustlings and scurryings. She kept looking around for the source of the sounds, but found nothing there. It was silence that stirred the hair on the back of her neck and made her wish Cole were behind her, instead of ahead, leading the way.

Though she had to admit, as she settled her gaze comfortably on the horse and rider ahead of her, that watching him was infinitely preferable to being watched by him. She found herself searching for words to describe him, but nothing satisfied her. Everything seemed either clichéd or subtly wrong. "Lean." Lean and hard were probably the most overused descriptive words in romantic fiction. Besides, "lean" always made her think of a cut of beef. "Slender." Too effeminate. "Lanky." He was undeniably lanky, but she'd always disliked that word. Rhymed with hanky. The word had a limp, lackadaisical sound. If Cole was lanky, he definitely brought a whole new meaning to the word!

The problem was, she kept getting his screen image tangled with the real one. In person, he seemed both smaller and more substantial than he did on the screen, and that contradiction both puzzled and excited her. The size difference wasn't hard to understand—movie stars were made to look bigger than life. Cole's on-screen movements tended to be flamboyant, swashbuckling; in person he moved with economy if no less style, his body language reflecting his natural reserve. But as for the other . . .

Katie knew very well that a screen image was only colored patterns on celluloid, projected across space on a beam of light. The artists responsible for creating those images used a different technique than she did, but the end result was to provide food for the insatiable human imagination. They did it with light and sound, she did it with printed words, yet the product was the same: illusion. But Cole Grayson was no illusion. He had touched her, held her body in his arms;

she had felt the heat of his body, felt his breath on her skin, felt his heartbeat against her own chest. Cole was human. He was muscle and bone and sinew. Cole was real. That fact had come to her with all the subtlety of an avalanche the night before in her tent, when she had suddenly found herself wondering what it would be like if he kissed her. Cole was real, and he was a man, and for some reason Katie found that frightening.

She was so lost in troubled musings that she didn't notice, at first, that her horse was slowing down. When he shuffled to a full stop and lowered his head to sniff the ground, thereby yanking the reins out of her hands so that she had to lurch clumsily over the saddle horn to grab for them, she observed that Cole had stopped, too, and was frowning at a log that was lying across the trail.

"Must have come down last spring, during the thaw," he said, glancing at her. "Don't remember its being here before."

"So what do we do?" Katie asked, feeling grumpy for no obvious reason.

Cole leaned an arm across his saddle and looked up to where the tree's exposed roots reached like a giant claw toward a pile of granite boulders. On the downhill side of the trail, the tapering end disappeared into a deep ravine. He said, "Go around it, I guess," and, making a clicking sound to his horse, turned tightly on the narrow trail so that he was facing Katie, his knee almost brushing hers. "It's too steep and rocky here—we'll have to backtrack until we find a way around this gully."

"Backtrack?" Katie tried to keep the dismay out of her voice. Her saddle sores weren't bothering her—yet— but she'd already been on this bloody horse longer than she wanted to. The only thing keeping her going was the thought of that lovely soak in a tub of hot water. To have to turn around and head back the way they'd come, for God only knew how far— No. It was unthinkable. "Isn't there," she ventured, swallowing hard, "any other way? Maybe if we got off and led them . . . ?"

Cole shook his head. "Too dangerous. We'd be better off trying to jump it."

"Jump it!" Katie grabbed at the idea the way she'd grabbed for the loose reins a moment earlier. "Why not? Couldn't we do that?"

Cole just went on shaking his head. Laughter was warm in his eyes. "Katherine . . ."

"Why not? I've seen horses jump things a lot higher."

"Sure," Cole said, the laughter moving into his voice. "It's no problem at all for the horses. It's you I'm worried about. No offense, darlin', but can you really see yourself jumping that log?"

"No," Katie said coldly, stung by the gentle derision in his laughter, "but then, I'm not planning to jump it. The horse does all the work. All I have to do is keep from falling off—right?"

"Yeah, that's about the size of it. Look, Katherine—"

"I think," she informed him, ignoring the quivery feeling that was beginning in the upper part of her stomach, "that I can manage to do that, if the horse does what it's supposed to do. You go first—show me how it's done."

Pride, she reflected morosely, was going to be her downfall someday. Pride and a competitive nature. By being so damned certain she couldn't do it that he hadn't even suggested the possibility to her, Cole had quite simply made it imperative that she do it or die trying.

"Katherine . . ." Cole said her name on an exhaled breath, holding her gaze. The warmth hadn't left his eyes, but had become something subtly different, something sharper, more intense. Again, as they had the night before in her tent, perceptions narrowed until Katie had the impression she was looking through a tube. The shivers in her stomach spread outward into her muscles.

Cole nodded abruptly and nudged his horse forward,

pressing his leg against hers as he leaned to grasp her reins. "You hold the reins like *this*," he said tersely, showing her. "Not too much slack, but don't try to interfere with him. Lean low over his neck—get your center of gravity as low as possible, understand?" He looked into her eyes, so close, she could see the tiny flecks of gold in his brown irises. She nodded without blinking. "And *hang on*." He slipped past her, muttering again about the inherent intractability of redheaded women, and moved off down the trail, back the way they'd come.

Katie watched him for a minute or two and then pulled clumsily on her own horse's rein and followed. When she came to a wide enough place in the trail she moved over and stopped. With nervous anticipation skating through her, she sat waiting.

A little farther down the trail Cole had stopped and turned. Katie saw him lean forward and say something, then gently slap the side of Diablo's neck. The horse broke into a sedate gallop.

When they passed her, Katie knew that the horse's unhurried pace was deceiving. She had a brief impression of heat and power, of a thunder in the earth beneath her, and then the huge animal gathered himself and rose into the air with effortless grace, clearing the log with room to spare.

There was a muffled grunt as they landed, then the clatter of shod hoofs on hard earth, the creak of leather, the jingle of metal. As he trotted back to the log, Diablo was tossing his head and tugging at the bit as if to say, "That was a blast—let's do it again!"

The whole thing hadn't taken thirty seconds. Cole was leaning across the pommel of his saddle, a little half-smile on his lips. "Okay, ma'am, your turn."

Katie muttered, "I think I've changed my mind."

Cole's smile broadened. "What was that? Don't think I quite caught what you said."

"Nothing!" Katie barked, and turned the buckskin's head to the trail. I'm crazy, she thought. If I insist on going through with this, I am truly crazy. And then she reminded herself, as she always did when she was about to do something foolish or frightening, that it was all grist for her creative mill. What didn't kill her, sooner or later wound up in a book. . . .

At the spot where Cole had stopped, Katie turned her horse around. Following Cole's example, she leaned forward and patted the buckskin's scruffy neck and muttered, "Okay, horse—do your thing." Taking a firm grip on the reins with one hand and the saddle horn with the other, she whacked him in the ribs with her heels.

The animal seemed surprised, but broke into a trot. Katie kicked him again, harder. He sort of stumbled into a gallop. Katie was suddenly reminded of the time she'd caught a wave, quite by accident, with her brother's surfboard. She remembered hanging on for dear life, feeling all that power beneath her, knowing it wasn't anything she could control or direct, watching in helpless panic as the beach rushed toward her. Just as that log was lurching toward her now. At the last minute, remembering what Cole had told her about her center of gravity, she leaned forward and shut her eyes.

But instead of becoming airborne, the horse, defying the laws of physics, came to a sudden and complete stop. Katie, obeying the laws of physics, kept right on going. In one clean, graceful movement she slithered over the animal's neck, described a neat semicircle in the air with her body, and landed on the ground in a sitting position, still holding the reins in one hand.

"Katherine?"

She heard Cole swear and call her name, but didn't feel much disposed to answer. When he called again, on a rising note of alarm, she uttered a brief, sibilant oath, flopped back full length on the ground, and covered her eyes with her arm.

From the other side Cole couldn't see her. He hadn't been able to see her, in fact, since she'd left the saddle. Which probably explained the way he came vaulting over the log, and the wild-eyed look on his face. As he dropped to his knees beside her he tentatively put out his hands, almost afraid to touch her, and whispered, "Katherine?" From under the barrier of her arm she watched concern etch tiny lines around his eyes. "Are you all right?"

She moved her arm and glowered up at him. Relief deflated his chest. He thumbed his hat back and rested his forearm across one knee.

"Nothing broken?"

"Just my pride," Katie said gloomily, putting the arm back over her eyes. "It's been taking a real beating lately."

"They say humility's good for the soul. Come on—I'll help you up."

"Why?"

"Because," Cole said patiently, confirming Katie's dark suspicions, "you've got to get back on your horse."

"Somehow, I was afraid you were going to say that. The ancient code of the horseman—if you fall off, you have to get right back on?"

"Way I see it," Cole drawled, "you haven't got much choice. Come on—up and at 'em." He took her hand and tugged her into a sitting position. She winced, and muttered "Ouch!"

"Bruised pride?" Cole inquired, deadpan.

Katie tried to glare at him but found it disquieting to scowl at a face that had captured millions of hearts. She shifted the scowl to the stupid horse, who was more deserving of it anyway. "Okay," she said, taking a deep breath, "what did I do wrong?"

Cole shrugged. "Wasn't so much what you *did*, as what you *are*."

"I beg your pardon?"

"A horse knows when he's got an inexperienced rider on his back. Some horses are sympathetic—they'll try to be gentle. But you get a horse with a mean streak, like ol' Jackson, here, and he'll get away with anything he can. You just have to let him know who's boss, that's all. Now, this time—"

"Whoa," Katie said, holding up a hand like a traffic cop. "Hold on just a darn minute. What do you mean, 'this time'? If you think I'm giving that beast another chance to splatter my brains all over that log—"

"Come on, Katherine. If we're going to the hot springs—"

"I've changed my mind," Katie said stubbornly. "I had a bath yesterday."

Cole gave a put-upon sigh and took off his hat. He looked down at it, then back at Katie, turning loose on her the most potent, high-voltage, blue-ribbon Cole Grayson smile he could muster. If Katie had been wondering how it would affect her when she was in full possession of her faculties, now she knew. It was like having a small whale frolic inside her chest.

As if that weren't enough to demoralize her completely, he reached out his hand to touch the side of her face, brushing a smudge from her cheek with his thumb. Realizing her mouth was hanging open, she closed it, then opened it again to allow her tongue access to her dry lips. They tasted dusty. "Hmm," she said carefully.

"Tell you what." He was still touching her face, still smiling that devastating smile. "If I ride poor old Jackson over the log, will you get back on him, and come with me to the hot springs?"

She thought, Cole, if you touch me, if you smile at me like that, I'll ride the wretched horse to the moon. . . . What she said was, "Um . . ."

Cole just chuckled and stood up, then helped Katie to her feet. "You climb on over and wait for me. Take Diablo's reins and move him out of the way for me, okay?"

She nodded, feeling dazed, and began to make her way to the log barricade. Then paused, stifling a hiss. When she proceeded, she moved much more slowly and carefully—hobbling, almost.

A moment later she found herself swept up and into a place that was beginning to feel almost like home to her—Cole's arms. Her first impulse was to put her arms around his neck, and since there really wasn't any other place to put them, she yielded to it.

"I'm fine," she murmured without much conviction. "You don't have to do this."

"Well," Cole drawled soothingly, "I know how painful wounded pride can be." His voice sounded furry, like something a person might like to cuddle up to. "You know," he added thoughtfully as he placed Katie gently on top of the log, "you're battin' a thousand, darlin'. Three for three. Three days I've known you, three disasters, three times I've had you in my arms. Katherine, I've got to tell you—there are less painful ways to do this."

For the life of her, she couldn't think of a reply. All she could do was sit like a bump on a log, literally, and watch Cole stoop to retrieve his hat, whack it a couple of times on his pant leg, and hand it up to her. He was grinning, a lopsided, all-American Huckleberry Finn grin. It was impossible not to grin back. And so, almost inevitably, the look became prolonged, became more than a look; became an acknowledgment.

Cole broke the contact first, abruptly turning to reach for Jackson's reins. "Okay, jughead," he said with a grunt as he swung himself gracefully into the saddle, "let's get this over with. I sure am lookin' forward to a nice hot bath and an Eskimo Pie."

"*Eskimo Pie?*"

"Yeah—didn't I tell you they had ice cream at the hot springs?"

"No, you didn't—if you had I'd have gotten that nag over the log on the first try!"

Cole's answering laughter followed her as she hopped down from the log and picked up Diablo's reins. She barely had time to move out of the way before she heard the drumming of hoofbeats and a blood-curdling *"Yee haw!"* She turned to look just as Jackson came bounding over the log as if he had springs on the bottoms of his feet, ears back, looking wild-eyed and affronted. Cole was looking smug.

As he was helping her to remount, Katie paused with one foot in the stirrup to whisper skeptically, "Eskimo Pie?"

"Uh-huh," Cole murmured, eyes full of promise.

"In that case"—Katie groaned, hauling herself into the saddle with the aid of a hefty boost from Cole—"point this beast toward that hot springs and get out of my way. Last one in the tub's a rotten egg!"

Although, as Cole had told her, the hot springs was located on the main backpacking trail that ran north and south through the Sierra Nevadas, it was hardly a bustling resort. It did boast a generator, which supplied the power for the cold box and deep freeze, but Katie wondered at the logistics involved in keeping those appliances stocked. Here, unlike Cole's camp, there was no handy meadow for helicopters to land in.

A small party of backpackers was resting on the cool, shady porch. They looked tanned and healthy. It gave Katie a jolt to see them—they looked so modern, with their brightly colored nylon backpacks and T-shirts with writing on them, reminders that out there beyond the time-warp world of the cow camp, the twentieth century was waiting. . . .

She got another jolt from Cole's reaction to the hikers. When he saw them he casually tilted his hat forward so that it hid his face in shadows. After tying Diablo and Jackson to the log railing in front of the store, he took a bandana out of his pocket and mopped his face and neck with it. As he mounted the split-log steps and crossed the porch, it just happened to be covering most of his face. . . . The actions were unhurried and completely natural—not even the most astute observer would have noticed anything unusual or evasive. But neither would that most astute observer have recognized one of the most famous faces in the world.

Incredible—it actually took that incident to make Katie realize that the man she was with was one of the most famous people in the world! It made her feel disoriented, somehow.

A thin, wiry man with curly gray hair and a tooth missing in front came down the split-log steps, smiling at her. He told her "Howdy," and supplied the information that his name was Ray, and that he'd be glad to show her to a bathhouse. He led her down a steep slope, fiddling busily with a bunch of keys on a length of rawhide, then unlocked a padlocked door, warned her not to doze off in the hot mineral water, and left her.

The bathhouse had a rough plank floor and was just big enough to accommodate the galvanized tin tub set into a box made of split logs. There was a wooden peg on the inside of the door, and a drop-latch closing. A single tap in the log wall at one end of the tub opened to emit steaming water and a strong odor of sulfur.

As she undressed, Katie noticed that the sores on her legs were almost completely scabbed over, and that in spite of having just spent the morning in the saddle, they didn't hurt at all. With an unexplainable sense of happiness and well-being, she lowered herself into the soothing water and lay back, letting her hair fan around her shoulders with a subtle, feathery caress. As her body relaxed, her mind drifted, and she found that it was repeating two words endlessly, over and over: *Cole Grayson Cole Grayson Cole Grayson. . . .*

Cole was leaning against the log wall of the bathhouse, eating his ice-cream bar. He was beginning to wonder if he was going to have to eat hers too—it was melting fast—before she came out.

She finally appeared, with a towel wrapped around her head like a turban, and a flushed, sleepy look on her face that struck him as incredibly sexy. She said, "Hi," when she saw him, and her voice sounded sexy too . . . low and husky. He held out her ice cream and muttered, "Eat it quick. It's melting."

She murmured a thank you and set down her saddlebag carefully between her feet before taking the ice-cream bar from him. Getting the paper off seemed to require her entire attention for a while, and when she finally bit into the soft ice cream, a big slab of the chocolate coating broke loose.

"Oops!" she said, as she tried to catch it before it slipped off, but instead Cole reached out and caught it with the end of his finger. When he offered it to her, her eyes opened wide. She stared at him for a second or two, then dropped her lashes so they hid her eyes, and took the chocolate from his finger. For one brief moment he felt the warmth of her breath, the softness of her lips and tongue, like a moth alighting on the tip of his finger.

"Mmm, *messy*," she said, laughing, moving away and using her hands to shield her face from him.

My God, Cole thought; she's *shy*. With men, at least. When he'd told Snake that, he'd just been making excuses to explain her absence from the cookhouse, but now he thought he might have hit the nail right on the head. K. T. Winslow might be the reigning queen of romantic fiction, but when it came to the real thing she was as shy and uncertain as an adolescent! It made a lot of sense, now that he thought about it—that way she had of not meeting his eyes sometimes, and the fear and confusion he'd seen in hers. She was free and easy with words, but it was nothing but a smoke screen.

She'd finished her ice cream and was looking for a place to dispose of the paper wrapping. Cole was so intrigued by his recent discoveries that he just stood with his arms folded, watching her with bemusement. What she did was crumple up the paper, stoop to un-buckle her saddlebags, and fastidiously tuck the litter inside. When she straightened, she was licking her fingers. Her face was more flushed than ever—that blush again. He couldn't believe it. He grinned in pure delight.

She gave him a look that was half uncertain and half resentful, as if she couldn't quite decide whether he was laughing with her or at her. She was still watching him as she lifted her arms to undo her turban; then she bent forward to let it fall around her face. Her eyes were dark . . . wary, like some sort of wild creature watching an intruder from a hiding place, trying to determine whether it meant danger to her or not.

Cole wasn't sure what she'd consider dangerous, but he had an idea his thoughts would do wonders for her blush, if she could read them. Every move she made did things to her soft cotton shirt that reminded him she wasn't as thin as she looked, not where it counted.

He suddenly cleared his throat and levered himself up onto a fallen log, shifting to find a comfortable spot on the rough bark. "The men are startin' to wonder about you," he said.

"Oh, really?" She paused in the middle of toweling her hair to give him a startled look. "Why?"

"Seems they can't decide whether you're stuck up or just shy," he drawled, "seein's how you haven't seen fit to show your face in the cookhouse since the day you arrived."

"Stuck up," she said dryly. "Definitely. Sure couldn't be anything like embarrassment, not after that little episode at the creek yesterday."

"Far as I'm concerned," Cole said very softly, "that's something that's just between you and me."

They traded looks for a few seconds, and then she lowered her eyelashes and murmured, "Of course—I'm sorry. She knelt down to take a hairbrush out of her saddlebag.

When she straightened, he said, "Come on up—the sun feels good," and held out his hand. She only hesitated a moment before accepting it, which made him feel as if he'd scored a minor victory.

And then for a while he just sat, basking and watching her brush her hair, watching the way the muscles moved in her forearm, the tendons in her wrist, the cords in her neck, watching the sun touch her hair with crimson light. The sun scorched his shoulders through his blue chambray shirt, while pine-scented breezes blew cool through his damp hair, then teased a few dry strands of hers.

"Pretty hair," he murmured, reaching out to touch a curl that had fallen inside the neck of her shirt. He inserted one finger between her skin and the strand and lifted it, weighing it, rubbing it between his thumb and fingers like fine silk. Then, with one finger, he deftly wove it back into the rest. Her hair smelled of apples, her skin looked fresh and clean, her lips looked warm and soft and full. . . .

The silence was profound; he *felt* rather than heard an inaudible humming and recognized it for what it was—sexual communication on a level more primitive than sound. He *knew* she was receptive to him, as certainly as if she'd issued a spoken invitation. The openness of her response was augmenting his desire to kiss her, making it something stronger. Making it *need*. He felt it like something heavy in the pit of his stomach, something that grew and throbbed with every beat of his heart. And he savored the weight of it, exulted in every pulse, because it had been so long since he'd felt anything so simple and uncomplicated as desire.

Except that for him, nothing could ever be simple and uncomplicated. This couldn't be just a case of a man and a woman. He wasn't only a man—he was Cole Grayson.

His vague reservations of the night before solidified and became the cold gray burden of his responsibility—some would have called it "honor." Whatever they called it, it meant he couldn't allow himself to kiss Katherine Winslow, because he knew he wouldn't want to stop at that. Casual sex was one thing with someone who knew the rules of the game, but this woman . . . amazingly, in spite of her age and a veneer of sophistication, this woman didn't. Not yet. Of course, if she hung around his world long enough, she'd learn. If she was going to write about him, she'd have to, but he wished with all his heart that she didn't.

"Pretty color," he said, his voice sounding distant and froggy, even to him. "Not quite a sorrel . . . more like a bay."

Five

Katie said, "That's some kind of horse, isn't it? As in, 'I'll put my money on the bobtail nag, somebody bet on the—' "

" '—bay.' Right. Dark red, black mane and tail."

"Hmm. Wonderful."

"What's the matter?" Cole asked, smiling.

"Nothing. Considering the way I feel about horses, I'm trying hard to consider that a compliment." Which wasn't what she was doing at all. What she was trying hard to do was quiet the panic that felt like a herd of butterflies stampeding through her chest. "I suppose," she added on a brave ripple of laughter, "I should consider the source." She let the brush lie still in her lap, because she felt that if she lifted it, her hand would shake, and that would betray her foolishness.

"Yeah, you could," Cole drawled as he took the brush from her slack fingers. "Or you could reconsider the way you feel about horses. Here, turn around."

She did, torn between dismay and relief. Dismay because of what he meant to do and the havoc it was going to play with her insides, and relief that at least he wouldn't be able to see the havoc written all over her face.

If she wrote this, she thought, her editor would blue-pencil it on the grounds that no one would believe it. She didn't believe it.

After carefully clearing her throat she managed to ask, "What do you mean?"

She felt Cole's fingers slip under her hair, felt them lightly brush her neck as he gathered the whole sun-warm weight of it into one hand. She closed her eyes, but that was a mistake. Because now, with Technicolor clarity, like film images projected on the backs of her eyelids, she *saw* his hands—hard, brown, callused hands, long, graceful fingers with magic in their touch. . . .

"You say you don't like horses. Ever stop to consider why that is?"

"No," Katie said. "I just don't, that's all."

"Katherine," Cole said gently, "that's bull. You don't just up and decide to dislike something. You generally dislike things out of ignorance or experience. Which is it—experience? Did you fall off a horse when you were a kid, or something like that?"

Katie snorted. "The first time I was ever on a horse in my life was day before yesterday, a real banner day for me."

"Okay, then, maybe you tried to pet one and it bit you."

"Sorry," Katie said, laughing.

"So," Cole said softly, "it's ignorance."

"Not anymore," Katie said darkly. "In the last two and half days I've acquired a wealth of experience."

"Oh, hell," Cole said cheerfully, "don't condemn a whole species because of old Jackson. I can see I'm going to have to educate you in the sensual joys of horseback riding."

"*Sensual?*"

"Sure. As a romance writer that's something you ought to be able to appreciate."

"Oh, I appreciate it, all right. Let me see, in the past couple of days, what 'sensual joys' have horses given me? Rubbed my skin raw—"

"Not fair. The saddle did that."

"Dumped me on my backside in the dirt, made me itch and smell bad—"

"Consider this," Cole said softly. "You're mounted bareback on a beautiful black stallion, racing through a meadow with the sun on your back and the wind in your hair. The air smells of grass and earth and pine . . . fresh and sweet. Your hair is loose, like the horse's mane; you can feel it on your neck. Your hands are tangled in the horse's mane . . . you're hanging on for dear life as the ground goes flying by . . . it's like riding the wind. There's nothing in the world like it—your heart is pounding, your blood racing, and between your thighs, all that power and energy. . . ."

There was silence. It grew thick and heavy before Katie managed to mutter, "It boggles the mind."

After that, for a time there wasn't any more talking. The silence was so fraught with awareness, it seemed overfull, as if adding words to it would cause a dam or floodgate to burst.

Gradually, imperceptibly, tensions relaxed and normal sensations returned. Katie could hear birds singing, a woodpecker tapping, distant voices. She felt the sun burning the top of her head, felt the brush drag through her hair in long, sure strokes.

He's done this before, she thought suddenly. Somewhere . . . sometime.

"Pretty hair," Cole said, sounding distant, almost clinical.

"I color it," Katie said, keeping her voice as flat and devoid of emotion as his.

"But it's your natural color, isn't it?"

"Yes, how did you know?"

"Just a guess." She could hear his smile. "You have a redhead's temperament."

"Ha! There's no such thing."

"Oh, yeah?" Soft laughter stirred the fine hair along her neck. "Did you take a lot of teasing when you were a kid? About your hair, I mean."

She shrugged. "I got teased, but I'm not sure my hair had anything to do with it. I had pigtails and glasses—"

"And freckles?"

"A few." She smiled.

"I thought you said—"

"I lied."

"Ah-hah." For a few minutes the only sounds were the rasp of the brush, the wind in the pines, and the dull echo of her own heartbeat. And then, without displacing those sounds, Cole murmured, "I wish I'd known you then. . . ."

There was a thickness in her throat, a tight, bitter ache. She swallowed it, and said, "You wouldn't have liked me. In addition to braids, glasses, and freckles, I was *plump*. And by the time I was a senior in high school and past the age for braces, my teeth had gotten crooked. I guarantee that guys like you never gave me a second glance."

Cole's voice became still quieter. "What do you mean, 'guys like me'?"

"Oh, you know." She tried a laugh, but the sound carried too much remembered pain. Cole's hands were still now, a warm weight on her shoulders. "The popular guys, the cool guys. The jocks. The studs."

"By which," Cole said evenly, "I suppose you mean the guys who were mainly interested in the size of a girl's—"

"Right. Another area, I might add, that in spite of my excess poundage I was somewhat lacking in."

Cole "Tsk'd," and murmured facetiously, "Poor baby." He'd begun to brush again, very slowly, with long sweeps that were almost caresses. "What *did* you have?"

"Brains . . . imagination . . . fantasies. Boy, did I have great fantasies."

"You know, Katherine," Cole drawled, "if you'd liked yourself a little better, I'll bet those 'guys' would have liked you better too."

"That's funny," Katie said, on another painful breath of laughter. "A counselor said the same thing to me once. I'll tell you what I told her."

"What's that?"

"That nobody ever told me it was *okay* to have braids and glasses and crooked teeth and freckles, and so on. I've got news for you—in this world, pretty is *in*. Homely is definitely *out*."

"So you decided you'd join the 'in' crowd—got rid of the extra pounds, along with a few more you probably should have kept—"

"That's a matter of opinion!"

"—ditched the braids. The glasses?"

"Unless I want to see."

"Uh-huh. The teeth—braces?"

"Right."

"The freckles?"

"Outgrew them, thank God!"

"But you kept the red hair. How come?"

The past, with its painful memories, had retreated before the triumphs of the present. Katie laughed easily now, a low ripple that felt good in her chest. "I found out that there's a big difference between being a redheaded kid and a redheaded woman."

Cole's laughter joined hers, and she reflected that there weren't too many things a man and woman could do together that felt better than sharing laughter.

"Well, darlin'," Cole said after a moment, "I think this mane of yours is about dry. What do you want to do with it?"

"Braid it!" Amid the warm rustlings of their laughter she reached back to take reluctant possession of her hair once more, but his hands gently denied her.

"Here . . . I'll do it."

"Mmm." Katie sighed, closing her eyes and letting her head fall forward. "That feels good." *She* felt good. She felt steeped in sunshine and pine-scented air, and in Cole's company. Amazing, how easy she felt with him—comfortable enough to let him know how good he made her feel. When had it happened? When had she begun to trust him? When had they begun to be friends?

"Cole," she murmured sleepily, lulled by his magical hands as he deftly worked an intricate French braid into her hair, "you amaze me, you know that? Where did you learn to do this?"

His hands became still. She felt him shrug, but he didn't answer, and after a moment he picked up a plait of hair and the rhythm of his hands resumed. Only, somehow, the joy and laughter had gone. Katie felt an inexplicable chill, as if the sun had dipped below the treetops.

"All done," Cole said suddenly, and dropped the end of the braid over her shoulder. "I don't know what you want to do about tying up the end." He picked up her brush and handed it to her. "We'd better be heading on back. I'll get the horses." He sounded distracted, but very, very gentle. He levered himself down off of the log and went striding up the slope, head down, his thumbs hooked in the back pockets of his Levis, leaving Katie confused, bemused, intrigued . . . and a little frightened.

Somehow, unknowingly, she'd hit Cole in a sensitive spot. More than sensitive. She'd touched a wound that had obviously never healed. He'd tried to hide his face from her, but she'd seen pain in the deep lines around his mouth, the long vertical grooves etched in his cheeks. It was interesting, to say the least, to find that Cole Grayson had painful secrets in his past, but that wasn't what Katie was thinking about as she watched him disappear into deep shade beyond the trees. She was thinking that only a few moments ago she had been feeling vibrant, alive, like a poppy blooming in the sun. Now it seemed that Cole was her sunshine; as he withdrew his warmth from her she felt herself closing up, the way poppies do when the sun goes down.

She found *that* very frightening indeed.

"You did that on purpose, didn't you?" Katherine said as they came in sight of camp. "You took a different way back so we'd miss that log."

Cole turned to look at her in surprise. "Yeah, I did. Why? Don't tell me you wanted to give Jackson another shot at it!"

"Not Jackson. Me. I wanted another shot at it."

He couldn't believe it; she actually looked disappointed. Shaking his head, he pulled Diablo up and waited for Jackson to shuffle to a stop beside him. Then he thumbed his hat back. "Why? You feel you have to prove something?"

"Something like that," she mumbled.

"You don't have to prove anything to *me*."

"All right. Me! Maybe I need to prove something to myself." She tipped her head and stared at him, looking stubborn as a mule.

"Katherine," Cole said, "do you think you could have jumped that log?"

She didn't answer right away, but took a minute to give it some thought. "Yes." She shook her head and said emphatically, "No. I don't *think*—I *know* I could."

"You believe that?"

"Yes!"

"Then why do you need to prove it?"

She was quiet again, thinking it over, then gave a funny little "Huh!" and smiled. He liked what a smile did for her face, and for her eyes. In this world, people smiled a lot, maybe too much, but not usually with the eyes.

"Oh, boy," Katherine said when they got close enough to camp to smell Birdie's cooking. "That sure smells good." She inhaled luxuriously.

Cole grinned at her. "Hungry, huh?"

"I don't know whether it's the riding, or the air up here, or that mineral water, but I'm *starving*."

"Oh, I'd say it's probably a little bit of all three," Cole drawled. "Listen, if you want to get off here and go wash up, I'll take Jackson—"

"Hey, no way." She grinned at him, and just for a second he caught a glimpse of the pigtailed urchin she'd been. "If I can jump this nag over a log, I can get the saddle off of him!"

Lady, Cole thought, I have an idea you could do just about anything you put your mind to.

He didn't tell her how to unsaddle a horse, and she didn't ask him. She just watched him and did everything he did, making him smile when she patted that jugheaded buckskin's neck and said, "Good ol' fella, good boy . . ." and even imitated Cole's gentling croon.

"How are your legs?" he asked her on the way down the hill. "That bear grease help?"

"Oh, yes." She threw him a grave look. "But you forgot to tell me about the side effects."

"Side effects?"

"Yeah—something's wrong with my legs. I keep doing this." She hooked her thumbs through the belt loops of her Levis and adopted a bowlegged swagger.

Cole's shout of laughter brought an answering grin that made him feel like hugging her. He restrained himself mainly because he didn't want to risk breaking the mood she was in; he was having too much fun sharing it with her. He didn't know where it had come from, but it was making him feel like a kid, and he hadn't felt like one in way too long.

The goofy mood followed them right into the cook shed. Cole went up to Birdie and gave her a loud, smacking kiss; it got him a not-too-gentle slap that left his cheek dusted with flour and biscuit dough.

"Hmm," he said, taking a piece of the sour dough from the breadboard, at the risk of losing his fingers, "what's for supper?"

"Stew." Birdie grunted. "And you can just keep your

fingers outa my biscuits—Cole, get away from there! What's the matter with you?" Cole had ventured to lift the lid of the huge pot that was simmering on the stove. Birdie snatched up a wooden spoon and whacked his knuckles with it, and he dropped the lid with a clatter.

"Ms. Winslow is hungry," he said, trying to sound aggrieved. Right on cue, Ms. Winslow's stomach gave a forlorn growl. She looked startled, and clamped one arm across her middle and the other over her mouth. Though she tried to look pathetic, he could see her shaking with stifled laughter.

"Huh," Birdie said, scowling suspiciously. "What did you have for lunch?"

Simultaneously Cole said, "Nothing," and Katherine said, "Ice cream!"

"*Her* I'll feed." Birdie sniffed, giving Cole a black look. "But you, you big ox, serves you right, ridin' all day without any lunch! Where's your brains?"

"Come on, Birdie, we're both starving!" He knew that would do it—Birdie couldn't stand the idea of anybody going hungry.

"Well . . . Okay, I'll make you a deal. You go get me some water and I'll make you a sandwich to hold you till suppertime. But don't you tell anybody, or I'll have men in here beggin' all day long! Those cowboys, they're *always* hungry! I swear—And don't take all day with that water, either! I need it for the coffeepot!"

By this time Cole had grabbed a bucket and Katherine's arm and they were both out the door, shaking with laughter. Birdie's voice followed them all the way down to the spring.

When she saw the spring, Katherine stopped and said, "Oh."

Cole moved around her with the water bucket, smiling to himself. He'd always thought it was a pretty nice spot, himself, and it pleased him that she seemed to agree with him.

Years ago Cole had built a wooden box over the upper end of the spring, both to keep animals and debris out of it, and to make it easier to draw water. On the lower end, where the water spilled over, it had created a small oasis of meadowland. The grass grew thick and spongy around warm pools of shallow water teeming with algae, insects, and tadpoles; watercress grew in the clear, cold trickle that ran away down to the meadow. And there were always flowers—sunflowers and filaree, dandelions and some pretty little blue things he didn't know the name of, and some cream-colored things he had an idea might be buttercups.

As he squatted on his heels on the wooden platform and lowered the bucket into the spring, Katherine moved to join him, picking her way gingerly across the marshy ground. She stood behind him, peering over his shoulder into the water.

Where the water reflected the sky it looked opaque, like blue plastic, but where her head and shoulders made a shadow she could see clear to the bottom. It seemed to fascinate her, as it had always fascinated him. The bubbling white sand had always reminded him of boiling porridge, and the water currents made moving patterns on the mossy rocks, so that they seemed to ripple like green silk.

Katherine's braid tumbled over her shoulder as she leaned over to gaze into the water. Cole didn't move out of the way, but watched her reflection as she caught it and held it against her neck with one hand. With the other she reached past him to dabble with her fingers in the spring. "Ow," she said, "that's cold."

She was very near. The front of her shirt brushed his shoulder; her words made warm puffs behind his ear. He could smell her hair, clean, sunny . . . like apples. All his senses felt sharp and raw; he felt restless and on edge, like having an itch he couldn't scratch.

Katherine gave a startled, breathy "Oh!" and drew back. A little greenish-brown frog had landed with a soft "plop" on the toe of her sneaker. Before Cole even had time to wonder what she was going to do about it, she had reached down and captured it in her hands.

"Well, well," Cole said, his voice catching on the edge of his laughter. "Katherine, you amaze me."

"Why? What did you expect, squeals of girlish dismay?" She had her hands full, literally, trying to keep the frog from wiggling out between her fingers. "Don't forget, I raised a future doctor. You wouldn't believe some of the things Christopher used to bring home."

"Guess I wouldn't." He had forgotten about the kids. She'd seemed almost like one herself, the past few hours. Still grinning, he turned and leaned down to pull up the water bucket. "What are you planning to do with him now that you've got him?"

"I'll think of something," Katherine muttered, and deftly dropped the frog inside the collar of Cole's shirt.

Six

For a second or two he couldn't believe it. He couldn't believe that Katherine Taylor Winslow, beautiful, elegant, an intelligent, full-grown woman, had actually done something so childish as to put a frog down his back! But she had. The damn thing was scrabbling around between his shoulder blades!

Shock receded before waves of emotion—a weird stew of emotions, actually, at least half of the ingredients of which he couldn't even identify. There were amusement, delight, surprise, indignation, even a touch of anger. But laced through it all, binding everything together, was a strange, unfamiliar *excitement*.

"Katherine," he said, keeping his voice very low and quiet, "take it out."

"Hmm?"

He turned slowly to look at her. She was standing with both hands clamped over her mouth, as if horrified by what she'd done. "I said, take it out."

"Cole—" Laughter burst through her hands. "Gee, I'm sorry. I don't know what got into me."

"Katherine, come here." It was hard to keep his voice stern and implacable when laughter and that peculiar excitement were quivering around inside him. "I know what got into *me*, and since you're the one who put it there, you're the one who's going to get it out."

"Cole . . ." She spread her hands helplessly.

"Come on. It's right there." He pointed to the spot. "If I move, it'll slip down farther. Hurry up."

She moved closer. He felt her touch his shirt collar. She made a breathy little sound, an embarrassed, frustrated sound, and reached timidly inside his shirt. "Geez," he said, "your hands are colder than the damn frog!"

"I'm sorry. I can't . . . seem to reach . . . far enough."

"The angle's wrong. Here, come around here." He pivoted on the ball of one foot and pointed to a spot directly in front of him. "Now, get down on your knees and reach over my shoulder and down my back. This'll make it easier." He unfastened the top two buttons of his shirt.

"Like . . . like this?" Her voice was shaking, but when she knelt in front of him he saw that she wasn't laughing anymore. She had her teeth clamped down on her lower lip, and he had an idea that if she let go of it, it would quiver. Her eyes were wide and very bright, like a child's; only the tiny lines in the fine skin around them reminded him she wasn't much younger than he was.

She put her hands on his shoulders. He could see her take a deep breath, bracing herself. She put her hand on his chest just below his collarbone, then slowly slid it up and over the curve of his neck and shoulder. Her hand didn't feel so cold anymore, just nice and cool. As she slipped it down between his shoulder blades she had to lean forward, so he put his hands on her waist to steady her.

"I can't find it," she whispered, sounding stricken.

"It's slipped," Cole said hoarsely.

"What shall I do? I don't think I can reach it." Her

eyes were closed. Cole could see a fine sheen of moisture on her skin. He could feel his pulse in his fingers where they touched her sides.

"The hell with it," he growled, and kissed her.

It wasn't a gentle kiss, though he'd meant it to be. He'd thought about kissing her, thought about what it would feel like, really *feel* like. He'd thought about the shape and taste and texture of her mouth and how he would feel with all his senses, not like this, like a hot knife twisting in his belly so he couldn't feel anything else at all. He couldn't enjoy the feel of her body in his arms, was hardly even aware of it. There was too much going on inside *him*. Chaos . . . insanity . . . *Insanity*. That was what it was. He was crazy. He knew he shouldn't be doing this. He'd told himself he wouldn't. But as far as he could see, he was probably going to go right on doing it for quite a while.

He pulled away from her experimentally, just to see if he had any willpower left at all. Her eyes were closed; when she opened them she looked dazed, as if she didn't know quite where she was. He brought his hand up to her face, touched it with the backs of his fingers, and brushed his thumb across her lips.

She whispered, "Oh, boy."

Cole said, "Amen," and lowered his mouth again to hers. So much for willpower, he thought.

He wasn't quite sure where it might have gone from there, if two things hadn't happened.

First of all, the frog, which he'd been ignoring, having slipped down as far as it could, was trying to get out of its predicament by making its way around the top edge of his Levis. When it reached the ticklish place at the side of his waist, Cole found that he couldn't ignore it anymore.

At almost that same moment, his work crew came home to supper, and as usual, the men weren't quiet about it.

When Katherine heard the racket she jumped like a teenager caught necking on the sofa. She actually said,

"Oh, gee whiz." Cole hadn't heard anybody say that in years. She put her fingertips over her lips and pulled away from him, and he was so distracted by the frog, he let her go.

She stood up, looking panic-stricken. Cole was swearing under his breath, tearing at his shirt buttons. She turned and stepped down from the wooden platform. "Katherine," he said, "wait a minute, dammit!" He started after her, pulling his shirttail out of his Levis as he went. She glanced around at him and her eyes went wide—and then, for some reason, she took off, running downhill, following the marshy ground beside the stream. Cole yelled, "Hey, come back here!" and took off after her. His shirt and the frog landed with a plop on the muddy grass.

She was wearing tennis shoes, so she had the advantage over him and his cowboy boots. But the ground was soggy, and treacherous with slippery algae. Just as Cole caught up with her, she lost her footing. He made an unwise attempt to stop the inevitable, and they both went down, sprawling, sending up a small geyser of muddy water that pattered down on them like warm rain. For a few seconds they just lay there breathing hard, her bottom under his belly, his face buried in the hollow between her shoulders. Then her shoulders began to shake. Cole let out a gust of laughter against her back. A moment later they were holding on to each other, rolling around, and laughing so hard, they could barely breath.

And how Katherine could laugh, Cole thought. He'd liked her laugh from the first time he'd heard it, and he found that the more she laughed the better he liked it. She didn't laugh like a lady—no dainty titters for her! She laughed out loud, she whooped, she chortled, she guffawed. It was the most contagious sound he'd ever heard, and for the first time in more years than he could remember, Cole laughed until his stomach hurt.

Katherine kept trying to say something, and eventually managed to gasp, "For this—for this we . . . rode fifteen miles to take a bath!" That set her off again, but she was trying to regain control now, so she smothered her howls against his chest. Cole wrapped his arms around her and held her, just held her, almost as if she were crying instead of laughing.

When they were reasonably calm again they helped each other to their feet, still breaking into fitful snickers and chortles, quickly controlled. Cole rested his arms on Katherine's shoulders, put his forehead against hers, and took a deep breath. She sighed. He pulled back a little, shaking his head.

"A walking disaster," he murmured, brushing at the mud on her face.

She made a settling-down kind of noise, and reached up to push the hair back from his forehead.

They stood there looking at each other, breathing in odd, jumpy rhythms. And suddenly something in the silence got to Cole. He shifted his focus, looking beyond her, then closed his eyes briefly, and said, "Uh-oh. Oh, hell. Katherine, we seem to have acquired an audience."

They were all there, his whole crew—Snake, Mendosa, Dwight, Sunday, Billy Claude, and about fifteen other men—standing below the cookhouse, in various stages of washing up, watching the show and loving every minute of it. Even Birdie had come out to see what was going on, holding a ladle in one hand and the lid to the stew pot in the other.

Cole's insides were already sore from laughing. Now they began to hurt with something else. He ached with pity for Katherine—she had so much pride, and after everything that had happened to her in the past couple of days, this would be about the last straw. He wondered if she'd ever forgive him.

After one quick, horrified glance around, she clapped her hand over her mouth and stared at him above it, her eyes big and bright.

"Katherine," he said gently, "I'm sorry. Why don't you go on back to your tent. I'll bring some hot water—"

"No." She sniffed, touched her nose with the back of

a mud-smeared hand, and shook her head. "No. I've been rude long enough. It's time I stopped acting like a prima donna, don't you think?" Her voice was soft, but firm.

Cole stared at her. She stood straight and tall, with her head up and shoulders back. Her hair was all out of its braid and full of grass and mud, she had mud on her clothes and splotches of it on her face, and her cheeks were flushed—whether from the exertion or embarrassment Cole couldn't tell. But he knew he'd never, in all his life and glamour-packed career, seen anyone look more magnificent.

She took a deep breath and wiped her cheeks with her hands, leaving muddy smears. "Well," she said, smiling at him, "aren't you going to introduce me to your friends?"

Cole looked at her for a minute, and then, without saying a word, offered her his arm. As they went up the slope together he was feeling humble. But much, much later, when he looked back on it, he thought that might have been the moment when he began to love her.

". . . Chipmunk, Pascoe, Billy Claude, Sunday Ochoa—he's the boss here—and Snake you already know," Cole said, completing the introductions.

Snake stepped forward and held out his hand. "That's Stanley, ma'am," he said with unexpected dignity. "Stanley Boggs."

"Stanley," Katie murmured. He had a nice, hard grip. All of them did. It came, she supposed, from handling rawhide and hemp and wild livestock all day long. They were also rather touchingly polite, like little boys trying to be on their best behavior. There was a lot of foot-shuffling and "How-do, ma'am"-ing—and trying not to grin from ear to ear. Katie had a quivery feeling in her chest, as if her fit of laughter hadn't quite expended itself.

"Well, supper's ready. You'd better get cleaned up,

the two of you," Birdie said sourly. "Forgot the water I asked you for, too," she muttered before she went back into the shed. But Katie had seen her huge body shaking with laughter as she turned away from them.

The men moved aside, making room for them at the washtub, then one by one shuffled off to the cook shed as if not quite certain whether they'd been dismissed or not. Billy Claude, the young kid with the shoulder-length blond hair, mumbled, "Ma'am?" and handed Katie a towel before going off to join the others.

"Nice guys," Katie said when she caught Cole watching her.

"Yeah, they are." He waved her to the washtub ahead of him. "Just don't expect them to treat you like one of the boys. They never heard of women's lib. They'll 'ma'am' you to death."

"I think it might be nice, for a change," Katie said, smiling at him as she rolled up her shirt sleeves. "I never did have anything against *being* a woman."

"Just against being *called* one," Cole said in a low voice that seemed to carry a new note of intimacy. The same special communion was in his smile, too, and in his eyes. The quivery feeling inside Katie acquired a sharp, vibrant edge. As she washed off the worst of the mud in the water from the galvanized washtub, she was thinking that if Cole Grayson called her "woman" in that tone of voice, and with that look in his eyes, she wouldn't mind it at all.

She moved back, drying her face and arms on the towel Billy Claude had given her, and Cole stepped up to the washtub. Katie didn't even bother to try not to stare at his naked torso. Here again, it wasn't that she hadn't seen it before; it was just so different seeing it in the flesh—literally. At once less and more. Smaller and more compact, but more dynamic, more vital. His body radiated heat and energy. It made her want to touch.

Inside her chest a whale turned a ponderous somersault. She buried her face in the towel as sensual memories overwhelmed her. Warm skin and firm muscle beneath her hands . . . vibrant masculine weight on her back, buttocks, and thighs . . . a mouth at once hard and tender . . . calloused fingers brushing her skin with a feather's touch.

Oh, boy. Taking a deep breath to restore sanity, Katie emerged almost fearfully from the towel, determined to make a more detached assessment of Cole's body. Lean and hard, of course. Naturally dusky but not especially tanned—cowboys didn't often work shirtless. He had no excess flesh, no softening around the middle, though his age did show in the silvering of body hair, which matched the silver at his temples. And he had several small scars, leftovers, Katie supposed, from his career beginnings as a stunt man and action extra.

"Well?" Grinning, Cole extended a dripping hand to claim her towel. "Let's hear it."

"Hear what?" Katie felt breathless and naked.

"*A Romance Writer's View of Cole Grayson,* by K. T. Winslow. Let's see, now—" A wicked gleam in his eyes, Cole lowered the towel and "ahem'd" portentously. " 'His lean, hard body, muscles rippling beneath sunbronzed—' "

"Egomaniac," Katie said, and snorted. "You're skinny, and except for your neck, you look like you crawled out from under a rock! I don't know how you've managed to fool the public all these years!"

Cole's grin broadened irrepressibly. "Makeup and special effects, what else?" The glint in his eyes softened and became that private communion. The grin faded. Slowly he reached out to brush her cheek with the towel, then draped it over her shoulder. "I'm no hero, Katie," he said softly. "Just a man." The smile came again to hover at the corners of his mouth, but didn't quite reach his eyes. "Right now, a *hungry* man. Shall we go see if that stew tastes as good as it smells?"

The stew was delicious. Katie ate two platefuls. She didn't know when she'd ever been so hungry. She also ate several—she lost track of how many—baking-powder biscuits with butter and honey, and then, after declaring she couldn't possibly eat another bite, polished off a huge piece of apple pie, still warm from the oven.

A little silence had fallen over the cook shed when she and Cole had first joined the men at the long trestle tables, but conversation soon picked up again. Katie's presence didn't seem to inhibit them, except that when one of them uttered a word stronger than "darn," he invariably said, "Pardon *me*, ma'am!"

Now and then one of the men would make a good-natured, teasing comment about Katie's intent to write a book about Cole. Neither his fame nor the fact that he was technically their employer seemed to impress them very much. They respected his skills as a horseman and cowhand, but his celebrity seemed to amuse them, as much as anything. Katie was beginning to understand why Cole kept coming back to this place, where the only thing that counted was how fast he could build a loop in a length of rope and get it around the neck of a wild steer. Where the only way to earn a man's respect was to put in an honest day's work. Where he was just plain Cole.

I'm not a hero, Katie. Just a man.

After supper, several of the men got a poker game going at the far end of the cook shed. Two or three others stayed at the tables to read paperback novels or write letters in the pool of light from the overhead lantern, and one—Chipmunk, Katie thought—got out a little pocket sewing kit and sewed a button on a blue chambray work shirt. Billy Claude got his guitar and went out to the campfire, and after an exchange of looks, Katie and Cole got up and followed him.

The campfire was in the center of a large cleared area, relatively level and ringed by logs. Within the ring, each man had his bedroll, and that bedroll was his private space. Already a few of the men were stretched out with their hats over their eyes, a duffle bag for a pillow, while others smoked or talked in soft voices or just sat staring into the fire or up at the sky, watching the night come slowly down.

Katie sat on a log near Cole's bedroll, listening to Billy Claude. He played mostly sad country music, or folk songs such as "Blowin' in the Wind." Sometimes Snake joined in on a harmonica, and other times, when it was a song everybody knew, the cowboys sang along, but generally it was only Billy Claude and the guitar, their gentle sounds intruding on the quiet no more than the sparks from the campfire usurped the stars.

Billy sang "Scarborough Fair" and "The Boxer" and "Lemon Tree," and then everybody had a lot of fun with "Tom Dooley" and "Lucille." After that Katie asked for "You Are my Sunshine," and she and Billy Claude did the harmony while everyone else sang the melody. Then it was Billy again, doing a love song that always made her think of David, and her marriage . . . and the divorce.

The song always made her feel sad in a poignant and wistful way that was hard to define. Tonight it also made her feel lonely.

She glanced down at Cole, who was leaning back against the log with his eyes closed, his arms resting on his drawn-up knees. For a few minutes Katie just looked at him, studying his face in its unguarded state, trying to make herself see it with some objectivity. She couldn't do it, and looking at Cole only made her feel lonelier. She wasn't sure whether he was asleep or not. After a while she eased herself off the log, meaning to slip away without disturbing him.

"Turnin' in?" Cole's voice was a sleepy drawl.

"Yes." There was a tight, achy feeling in her stomach.

"I'll walk you."

"No," Katie said softly. "Don't get up. I can find my way."

"Sure?"

"Yes."

"Okay, then. 'Night, Katherine."

" 'Night"

Back in her tent, Katie turned on her lantern and fished her glasses, a steno pad, and a fine-point pen out of her briefcase. She sat cross-legged in the middle of her sleeping bag, staring down at the pale green paper. Her glasses slid down her nose. She pushed them back up. Then she folded her arms across her stomach and leaned forward, pressing on the hot, hard knot there. It began to throb, so she rocked with it, gently, back and forth. After a while she straightened, took a deep breath, and tried again to concentrate on the empty green tablet. Half an hour later she'd written "Cole's Men" on the top line.

"Self-discipline, Katherine," she said sternly, and, as fast as possible, scrawled a list of as many names as she could remember. "Snake"—she crossed that out and wrote "Stanley Boggs" instead. "Billy Claude, Chipmunk, Sunday, Mendosa, Pascoe, Roman, Stony Blue" —could that be right?—"Lenny, Will, and Frank . . ."

That was all she could remember—she never had been good at remembering names. But some of them were beginning to stand out, to separate themselves from the collective "cowboys," or "Cole's men," and become individuals. There was Snake, of course, and Billy Claude, a college dropout, younger than most of the others, with a kind of sweet idealism that reminded Katie of the flower children of the sixties. A child-man, born in the wrong age . . . And there was Chipmunk. Katie wondered how he'd come by that nickname—he didn't look anything like a chipmunk. Pascoe looked like a chipmunk, though, with his bald head, round red cheeks, and receding chin. And Sunday, the foreman, resembled a college professor, with his dark-rimmed glasses, intelligent eyes and quiet dignity.

By the time she put aside the notebook and glasses and straightened her cramped legs, she had filled a dozen or so pages with notes and thumbnail character sketches. It had been more an exercise in self-discipline than anything else, mental activity to keep her mind off Cole. But when she had turned off her lantern, undressed and pulled a sweat shirt on with her panties, and crawled into her sleeping bag, she knew it had been an exercise in futility. It would take more than a few pages of notes to take her mind off Cole Grayson.

He'd slipped under her skin, permeated her entire being, like a virus! And like a virus, there didn't seem to be any cure for it. She'd just have to let it run its course. Meanwhile she'd better get used to having him occupy her mind every waking and sleeping minute. She should have expected this, since she always fell in love with her heroes.

She lay in the dark, listening to the sound of the blood rushing through her veins, like the pounding of distant surf. She felt rigid, tense, chilled on the outside and hot inside. With a small sense of dismay she realized that she was listening for the sound of footsteps.

If she were writing this, she thought, she wouldn't be alone. If she were writing this, Cole would come to her now.

But she wasn't writing this. She was living it. Cole Grayson wasn't something she'd created—he was a real, living, human being. She couldn't control his actions, feelings, responses. She couldn't plan the dialogue, put the right words in his mouth. She couldn't guarantee a happy ending. And when it was over, she couldn't put him in the cupboard reserved for old manuscripts and forget him. Cole Grayson wasn't going to stop *being* when she stopped writing about him.

It was a long time before Katie fell asleep, and when she did it was with the refrain from an old song playing over and over in her mind. It was a song she'd known practically all her life, but was beginning to find very disturbing:

You are my sunshine, my only sunshine,
You make me happy when skies are gray;
You'll never know, dear, how much I love you.
Please don't take my sunshine away.

"Good morning, sunshine. Rise and shine."

Incredulously, sure she must be dreaming, Katie murmured, "Cole?" and put out her hand. She touched fabric, a shirt collar, then a jaw that felt cool and moist, as if it had just been shaved. She snatched her hand back and levered one eye open. "It's pitch dark!"

"Only in here. Out there in the big, wide world it's morning. A beautiful morning. Come on, get up. I want to show you something."

Katie sighed, and struggled to a sitting position. "What?"

"Uh-uh. You have to get dressed and come with me. And hurry up or we'll miss it."

Katie glared balefully at him, or, rather, at the slightly increased warmth and density he made in the darkness beside her. "Okay," she mumbled. "I'll get dressed. Go away."

"Nope. I can't see you anyway. What are you wearing?"

"Sweat shirt. Underpants."

"That'll do. Just put on pants and shoes. Where are they?"

"What *is* this?" Katie grumbled bitterly, groping for the Levis she'd taken off the night before. She was never at her best in the morning anyway, and certainly not before she'd brushed her teeth and had several quarts of coffee. And besides, she had a lifelong habit of associating morning with *daylight.* She'd have suspected Cole of playing some kind of practical joke on her, except that she could hear the racket the cowboys made as they saddled up and rode off to work. Katie decided Birdie was right—a man had to be crazy to be a cowboy.

"It's *cold*," she muttered, standing up to button her Levis.

"It'll warm up," Cole said cheerfully, and then, as she gave a massive shudder, he added, "Here, this might help." Something warm and heavy enveloped her. A parka. Fur-lined. Katie gave a grateful little chuckle and snuggled into it.

Outside the tent the air was so fresh and cold it tickled the nose and throat like chilled champagne. As she stood shivering, more from excitement than cold, she heard a soft whickering noise; a large black shape separated itself from the thinning darkness.

"Only one?" Katie said, straining to see beyond the shadows, looking for Jackson.

"Only one," Cole replied, a smile in his voice. She felt his reassuring touch on her elbow before he moved away. "Come up behind me," he said. "Give me your hand."

"I can't find the stirrup," Katie muttered, groping for it.

"No stirrups. Step on my foot."

She put out a hand and touched warm horsehide. It quivered slightly beneath her fingers. Moving them, she found the cold stiffness of denim. Then Cole's hand enveloped hers and she felt his muscles flex and become steel. A moment later, miraculously, she was sitting astride a broad, warm back.

"Put your arms around me," Cole said. "Hold tight. Hug his belly with your legs."

"Okay." She was laughing a little, wide awake now, and breathless with anticipation.

"Ready?"

"Yes."

She put her arms around Cole's waist and the horse began to move, slowly at first, a nice, steady walk. But when dawn had faded the darkness to twilight, Cole turned his head and murmured, "Hold on." He leaned forward then, spoke softly to his horse, and made a clicking sound with his mouth. Katie felt his body grow tense in her arms. Under her, powerful muscles gathered themselves and then exploded.

Katie said, "Oh, gosh," and pressed her face against Cole's back.

It was terrifying, exhilarating. It was beyond anything she'd ever known before. It was like riding the wind. She wanted to laugh out loud with the joy of it, but she was too frightened. Under her was thunder; the world flashed past in lightning bursts; the wind tore at her hair and snatched the breath from her lungs. All she could do was close her eyes and hold on to Cole, her anchor in the midst of the tempest.

"Katherine . . ." Her anchor spoke softly, with laughter in his voice. "You can let go now. We're here."

Katie opened her eyes. The light had a pearly translucence, like the inside of a seashell. "Where is here?" she asked huskily, testing her voice.

Cole just chuckled. He steadied her as she slipped down off of Diablo's back. Then he did the same, dropping the ends of the reins to the ground. He turned to her, smiling. "Did you like that?"

She nodded and stood hugging herself in the oversized parka, shaking all over, nodding her head, and laughing, sort of. And sniffling, because the cold wind had made her nose run. She wanted to shout, Cole, put your arms around me! Yes, that was wonderful. It was terrifying.

He didn't put his arms around her, but his smile grew warm with intimacy, and his voice was almost a caress. "Good," he said, and took her hand, guiding her as if they were crossing a ballroom floor.

They were on a large flat rock that jutted out over the meadow like the prow of a ship. Cole led her to the very edge and sat down, settling her between his knees. He started to put his arms around her, then pulled back. "Here, let me have that parka," he murmured.

"Oh, sure." She let him slip it off over her shoulders. He put it on himself, and wrapped it around them both.

She leaned back, feeling his cold front come against her warm back and begin to take in her body's heat. His face was cool against the side of hers; if she turned her head just a little, she would brush his lips with her eyelashes. She took shallow, careful breaths, trying not to lose herself in the intoxicating smell of fur and the clean scent of him. Shaving soap and woodsmoke and pine, man scents she'd almost forgotten. Her stomach grew quivery.

"What am I supposed to see?" she asked, though she didn't really care.

He pointed across the meadow. "Any minute now," he said, the words touching her temple. "Just watch."

It was so quiet that she could hear her own heartbeat, his breathing, the faint jingle of Diablo's bridle. Across the meadow, behind jagged pine-tree silhouettes, the sky was slowly turning from gray to a hundred shades of mauve, lavender, pink, and blue. And now, fragmented by the trees, she saw a thin sliver of fire. She could *see* that it was fire—it writhed and pulsed with heat and power. As it grew it hurled bolts of fire between the tree branches, like missiles from an angry god. Where the bolts touched the meadow they set it ablaze, turning dew to molten gold.

A bolt struck Katie in the face. She put her hand up to shade her eyes and whispered, "Oh." Beyond that there was no need for words.

Cole's hand tightened on her shoulder. He pointed once more, lower this time, down into the meadow, and now she could see them too—the little band of deer: a young buck, several does with their half-grown fawns. They'd been there all the time, grazing in the deep shadows at the edge of the trees. Now, as the sun's warmth touched them, they seemed overcome by a kind of giddy joy. It affected the young ones first. They began to hop and dance, then to chase one another in and out among the adults, who had stopped grazing to watch the antics of their offspring with placid indulgence. All at once the whole band erupted, leaping sideways, bounding over obstacles real and imagined, and finally disappearing into the trees like smoke on the wind.

"Well," Cole said, clearing his throat.

"That was some show," Katie said huskily, turning to look at him. "What do you do for an encore?"

Cole's eyes seemed to glow. It was suddenly too warm

in the parka. He tossed it back, stretched, and stood up. "How about some breakfast?"

"Breakfast?" Katie watched him lift saddlebags from Diablo's withers.

"Yep. Alfresco." He settled himself on the parka, took a thermos bottle out of the saddlebags, unscrewed the top, poured it full of steaming coffee, and handed it to her. She sipped, then handed it back.

"Mmm, that tastes good. What else?"

"Try this." He handed her an egg, bacon, and biscuit sandwich wrapped in aluminum foil, still warm. It was delicious. Katie ate two and Cole ate three, and they split the last one. They shared the coffee, too, passing the cup back and forth. When the thermos was empty, Cole packed it and the foil back in the saddlebags and stretched out on the parka, with the bags for a pillow.

When he caught Katie looking at him a moment later he sat up again and took off his shirt. "You told me I looked like I crawled out from under a rock," he drawled.

Katie delicately cleared her throat and looked off across the meadow. A bit prissy, she knew, but it was impossible to look at that body without wanting to *touch* it.

"Come here," Cole growled suddenly, and reached out to catch her hand and pull her down beside him. "Look." He was pointing again, straight up into the porcelain sky, using the arm that pillowed her head. He caught her head between that rocklike forearm and his other hand and tilted it to follow the direction of his pointing finger. "Know that line from *Oklahoma*? The one about watching a hawk?" His voice was lazy, almost sleepy. "I couldn't tell you how many times I did this when I was a kid, just stretch out somewhere and watch a hawk, listen to him cry. Ever hear a hawk's cry? Listen."

Katie listened. She heard the thin, far-away cry and thought it seemed terribly lonely. She listened to Cole's voice and felt hot and achy all through her insides. Her cheek rested against the smooth inside of his forearm; if she turned her head just a little she could touch it with her lips, taste it. Would she do it, she wondered, if he weren't Cole Grayson? *Yes!* she thought, but she knew that was only frustration talking. Because the truth was, she wouldn't have had the courage to do such a thing no matter *who* it was. Rejection was a very good teacher—its lessons were hard to forget. So Katie lay rigid and still, and listened.

Seven

Cole felt the slightest of tremors run through her body. And though he knew it was insanity, something in him cried out in primitive masculine triumph: *Yes! Yes! Respond to me!*

She was so stiff, so tense, lying beside him as if touching him would be a mortal sin. Yesterday she'd been so different—free and comfortable with him, like an old friend, sharing laughter and mischief. Yesterday, he thought, they'd been like children in Eden.

Yesterday, he'd kissed her. They'd eaten the apple. Today they were *aware*.

Cole took a deep breath, filling his chest as full as he could, trying to crowd out the knot that had settled in the center of it. What was going to happen between them was inevitable; he didn't think he could stop it even if he wanted to. He just hoped he could keep her from getting hurt too badly by it.

"When I was a kid," he said, making his voice a soothing, gentling murmur, "I used to find a private spot like this and lie for hours, watching the hawks.

And the turkey buzzards. They always fascinated me, the turkey buzzards. I used to wonder if they'd think I was dead . . . if they'd come and try to eat me. I thought maybe, if I lay real still, they'd come close enough for me to catch one."

"Ugh," Katherine said, shuddering. "Why would you want to?"

Cole sighed. "Ah, the poor, maligned buzzard. His cousin the condor gets all the publicity, gets to be a national hero, the mascot of lost causes. Little school-children give their pennies to the condor, but who loves a turkey buzzard? Nobody."

"Okay, okay!" She was laughing, and her laughter loosened her body and made her stir and turn instinctively toward him, as he'd known it would. He flexed his arm, giving her head a little squeeze.

"Cole," she said, tilting her head just a bit to look at him, "where were you a kid? Where did you grow up?"

"Hmm. Who wants to know—Katherine, or K. T. Winslow?"

She considered. "Both, I guess."

"Fair enough. I was born on a ranch down in the valley, about eighty miles from here as the crow—or buzzard—flies. Grew up there. The place is half mine, half my brother's."

"I didn't know you had a brother."

"Yeah, well, we're very different, Rob and I. Always were. But you see why these guys treat me the way they do. They're family. The older ones have known me since I was in diapers—Birdie, Sunday, Snake—we all grew up together. The younger ones I've known since *they* were in diapers—Stony Blue and Frankie, who are Birdie's nephews, by the way—everybody but Billy Claude. He just showed up one day, asking for work, and I liked his attitude, so I let him stay. Chipmunk and Pascoe—"

"Cole," Katherine said, poking him gently in the ribs, "I was asking about *you*. What kind of a child were you?"

"What kind of a child was I?" Cole laughed softly. "Dreamer . . . misfit . . . black sheep. My dad was a great guy. He was fair. Treated my brother and me just the same, or tried to. But Rob was the dependable one, the steady one, solid as they come, just like my dad. But me . . . well, I thought the ranch wasn't big enough to hold me. I always figured there was *more*, somewhere; the world was out there, waiting for me, and I wanted a bigger piece of it."

"You were right," Katherine said. "And you got it."

"Yeah." His chuckle made him feel as if there were sharp things flying around inside his chest. "I guess that's a clear case of 'Be careful what you wish for.' "

"Do you regret the way your life has gone? If you had it to do over again, would you do it differently?"

He shrugged. "I have regrets. And there are things I'd surely do differently, if I had the chance. But just about anybody you ask that question of would say the same. Wouldn't you?"

"I suppose so." She was silent for a minute or two, thinking about it, then tipped her face up to look at him. "But on the other hand," she said, smiling, "if I'd done anything differently—even just one tiny little thing—maybe I wouldn't be where I am right now."

"That's true. And you like where you are right now?"

"Yes." Her voice was low, husky. "I do."

His heartbeat grew hard and heavy. A strand of her hair tickled his face. He caught it and held it up where he could see it, feeling its texture with his fingers. He had a sudden urge to bury his hands and face in it.

"Sorry," she muttered, reaching up to take the strand from him. "It's all over the place. God, I must look like such a—"

"Katherine, you worry too damn much about what you look like."

She gave a short laugh. "Well, shouldn't I? It's kind of important."

"Not that important."

"Cole, you, of all people—the business you're in—you *know* how much it matters what a person looks like!"

"Maybe," he said quietly, "that's one of the things I don't like about the business I'm in."

"All right," Katherine said after a moment's thoughtful silence. "But it's a fact that appearances *are* important, no matter what business you're in. I could give you a thousand examples, but you already know I'm right."

"I guess I'm talking about personal relationships. Beyond first impressions, do you really notice what the people closest to you look like? Beauty only gets in the way of relationships. People expect certain things of you based on what you look like, and that might not have anything to do with who you really *are*."

There was a little silence, and then she reached up to touch his face. "I'm sorry. I guess you would know about that better than anyone." And then, hesitantly, she asked, "Cole? Why haven't you ever married?"

He tried hedging. "Who wants to know—Katherine, or K. T. Winslow?"

"Me, I guess. Just Katherine."

"Never met anyone I felt like marrying, I suppose."

"All the beautiful women you've been associated with—"

"That's what I mean about appearances, Katherine."

"Then you've never been in love?"

Cole listened to the silence. In it, he heard himself answer, "I didn't say that."

He could feel her body become very still. "So you did love someone?"

"Yes. Once."

"But you didn't marry her."

"No."

"Why not?"

He shrugged. "It didn't work out. It was a long time ago. I was . . . very young."

Perhaps hearing something in his voice, she whispered hesitantly, "Do you want to talk about it?"

"No," he said, raising himself to look down at her. "Not now." And because it felt right to him, like filling a space inside himself that had been empty for a long, long time, he lowered his head and kissed her.

He was prepared for it this time, and so was she. He felt it all—the soft sigh of her breath, coffee-scented and warm; her lips, firm, but trembling a little with her response to him; her cheek, velvety smooth beneath the sensitive pads of his fingers. As her lips parted in acceptance of the gentle intrusion of his tongue, heat poured into his chest and expanded. He fitted his palm to the side of her neck, measured the thread of her pulse, and then slipped it around to lift and cradle her head.

The heat inside him became flame, hot and searing. He heard himself make a low sound, heard her response—communication on a level too primitive for words. He drew back a little, altering the angle, increasing the depth of the kiss. Their bodies shifted, searching for a better fit, a greater closeness. He felt her hand touch his face, then come around him to stroke his back. Felt it slide down until it met the waistband of his Levis, hesitate, then move slowly upward again. His own hand slipped down and under her sweat shirt to find the warm, smooth satin of skin.

It felt good. So good.

She drew in her breath at his touch, contracting her muscles, lifting her rib cage. He moved his hand back and forth, feeling the tautness of her belly, the hard ripples of her ribs, then filled his hand with the unexpected fullness of her breast. Trembling, she pushed against his hand.

Yes, he thought. *Want me!*

He wanted her with an elemental hunger, man for woman. No paper romances or celluloid heroes, just plain old desire, primitive and uncomplicated. He wanted her just like this, with nothing between them and the earth but animal skins, nothing over their heads but the sky. He wanted to fill his hands with the textures of her, his mouth with the taste of her, with the sun burning his back and the breeze cooling his sweat.

And he knew that she did want him, with an urgency as great as his own. Her skin felt hot; her body shuddered with wanting.

He withdrew from her mouth slowly, reluctantly. The fires inside him became something that writhed and twisted in his belly and left cold knots in all his muscles. He lay very still, cradling her body in his arms and gazing down at her face. She was so vibrant—crimson lights in her hair, cheeks flushed pink, lips ripe and bruised from his kiss—she made him think of exotic flowers, like hibiscuses, or poppies. Fresh, clean, sunwashed, wide open . . . and so very fragile.

Katherine, he thought. *Poor Katie.*

"Cole," she whispered, and then swallowed and said again, "Cole, I—"

He stopped her, touching her lips lightly with his own. "Shh . . ." Yes, he thought, she wanted him, or thought she did. He'd made her want him—or rather, he'd made her want Cole Grayson. Why not? Wasn't that what he did best? Wasn't that why he was so successful? He could make millions of women fall in love with Cole Grayson, so why should this one be any different?

I always fall in love with my heroes. . . .

He looked down into her eyes, so wide and somber, they seemed almost black. He forced a smile and said, "Well."

She murmured, "Some encore."

They sat up slowly, holding on to each other, but keeping a distance between them. When they were upright again, Katherine used both of her hands to smooth the hair back from her face, then left them there, as if she were trying to hold her head together.

Cole sat watching her for a minute. "Katherine, what are we going to do about this?"

She glanced at him, then away quickly. "There it is again," she muttered.

"What?"

"That cowboy drawl." She sounded irritated, but Cole thought he understood. He felt a bit testy himself. Frustration, he supposed.

"Sorry," he said gently. "I guess it's gotten to be a habit."

She snapped, "Don't be so darned agreeable!" And then smiled ruefully and murmured, "Sorry."

"That's okay."

For a while they just sat in silence, looking at each other.

"Katherine, it won't work, you know."

"I know," she said, and looked away, but he could see she wasn't buying it. She just didn't have the confidence it would take to argue with him.

As gently as he knew how he said, "It seems to me that we can have a relationship or we can have a *working* relationship. I don't see how we can do both, do you?"

"No, and I have contract commitments. My publisher, editors—not to mention my agent—will be very unhappy with me if I screw this up." She tried to smile, but it slipped awry. "So what do we do?"

"We were gettin' to be pretty darn good friends. You know, it's not just anybody I'd let get away with dropping a frog down my back."

She touched her lips with the tips of her fingers. Her laughter was a dark, husky sound. "Get *away* with it? You got even, in spades! I've never been so—"

"It was fun, though, wasn't it?"

"It was." She lifted her hand, touched the side of his face, almost touched his chest, then let the hand drop. In a voice that wasn't quite steady she said, "I have a book to write, and in order to do that I need to get to know my subject. I think there's still an awful lot to be learned about you, Cole Grayson. Do you think I can do that better if we're friends than if we're . . ."

"Lovers?" Cole finished softly. "Yeah, I do." He reached out to touch a strand of bright hair, then tucked it behind her ear. "Friends don't lie to each other. Lovers do."

He bent down to pick up his shirt, hiding his face from her because he could feel the twist of bitter memory on his lips. *And maybe, Ms. Winslow, when you've found out all there is to know about Cole Grayson, if we're still friends . . . if you still think I'm a hero . . . maybe then.*

On the way back to camp, riding behind him on Diablo, she tried hard not to touch him. He felt her there anyway, like a hot brand on his back.

It was Sunday. The next day Katie would have been in Cole's camp for a week. It seemed like a day.

It seemed like a lifetime.

The day before, the chopper had come in, bringing mail and supplies, including plenty of beer. The pilot, whose name was Sandy, had stayed on for an early supper. Afterward, since there was still plenty of daylight left, most of the men had gone off for a Saturday-night bathe in the creek. Cole, after giving Katie a private wink and a grin that turned her insides to custard, had gone with them. Katie had taken a bucket of water and retired to her tent. Cowboys might be crazy, as Birdie so often pointed out, but that didn't mean *she* was.

When she had finally emerged from her tent, scrubbed clean, smelling sweet, and dressed in a soft sweater and slacks, the chopper had left, and Cole with it.

Business in town, Birdie told her; he'd be back tomorrow.

Oh, Katie had answered, nodding, and had gone back to her tent, determined to get some serious writing done in his absence.

But though she knew it was childish, she couldn't help feeling abandoned. The sounds of music and laughter that drifted across the slope from the campfire seemed far away, and only made the night colder, darker, emptier. And once again, Katie had fallen asleep with the refrain from "You Are My Sunshine" echoing through her mind.

Please don't take my sunshine away . . . .

She had waked up this morning thoroughly disgusted with herself, and determined to regain some semblance of control and perspective. There wasn't any point in lying to herself—she'd spent too much of her life doing that, convincing herself and everyone else that everything was fine with her. But she'd learned the futility of lies—truth always caught up with you sooner or later—so she was admitting to herself readily enough now that she was falling in love with Cole Grayson.

And right on schedule, too. Except that this time it was different. She couldn't lie to herself about that, either.

Falling for a fantasy hero she'd created was one thing; falling for a real person was another. Her paper romances made her feel good, smug, and secure in the certainty of a happy and thoroughly satisfying ending. Neat and tidy, with no loose ends dangling, just the way her fans and editors demanded it.

But this . . . Right now she felt just plain awful. And wonderful. She felt alive—and scared to death. She felt happy just being around Cole. He could make her feel like singing, with that look that was specially theirs; melt her with that certain intimate timbre in his voice. And the moment she was away from him she felt uncertain. Lonely. And afraid. Because she just couldn't see how this was all going to turn out.

She couldn't *control* it! And she didn't like not being in control, not one bit. She'd worked too hard to get control of her own life. But right now she felt a little like she'd felt the morning Cole had taken her bareback riding at dawn. She was riding the tempest, and all she could do was shut her eyes tight and hold on, and hope she wasn't riding for a fall. . . .

After that morning, Cole had taken her to where the men were working cattle. It was hot, dusty, gritty, exhausting work. A man *did* have to be crazy to be a cowboy! Katie couldn't believe how hard the men worked. It was no wonder they rode into camp each evening famished, and fell asleep as soon as it was dark.

For all that, she might have found it boring as hell, too, if it hadn't been for two things. First, Cole gave her a job to do. It was her responsibility to tend the fire that kept the branding irons hot, and to hand over the vaccine syringes when they were called for. It wasn't long before she was as hot, dusty, and sweaty as the men, and the afternoon passed quickly. But even without that diversion, Katie didn't think she'd have noticed the passage of time. It was fascinating enough, just watching Cole.

All the men had the skills—they could ride, rope, wrestle a wild steer to the ground. But none of them could match Cole's effortless grace. Every movement he made was beautiful. Katie had seen bigger men, stronger men, men with big muscles and magnificent proportions, but Cole had something that was harder to define and impossible to deny. He had style. It was subtle and inherent. It couldn't be taught and it couldn't be disguised. It wouldn't diminish with age or the fading of physical beauty. It was what made Cole Grayson unique and unforgettable.

Unforgettable. How in the world was she going to forget him when the book was done?

A wave of longing washed through her, cold, salty, bitter. She felt as if she were missing something. Something concrete. Someone. She wanted someone to hold her, someone to hold on to.

Oh, Katherine, for heaven's sake, grow up!

The camp was quiet; most of the men had ridden off to Monache for a change of scenery, except for Billy Claude and Frankie. They'd taken Diablo and Frankie's favorite horse, a pinto mare named Suzie, and gone off on business of their own. Birdie was reading the Sunday papers Sandy had brought her. Katie spent the morning heating water on the big iron stove and washing her clothes, and then repairing the week's damages to her nails as best she could. At noon she made herself a sandwich out of homemade bread and leftover roast beef, and took it to her tent along with a huge mug of coffee. She was supposed to be working, after all, not dwelling on adolescent fantasies.

Adolescent, she reflected, was probably a good word for the way she was behaving. Right now her children were probably more mature than she was. Certainly Kelly, who had been serious-minded and goal-oriented even at eleven, would look at her with puzzled irritation and say, "Mother, don't you think you're being just a bit *silly* about this?" Chris, though—dear, sensitive, loving Christopher—he'd always had a romantic streak.

Resolutely Katie pushed her glasses up onto the bridge of her nose and opened her notebook to the pages she'd written the night before.

> "Lunchtime Saturday. Asked Cole about scars
> on Diablo's chest . . ."

It was Katie's second day out with the men, and she was beginning to feel like an old hand, one of the guys, stretched out in the shade of the pine trees, away from the heat, humidity, and insect life in the meadow. The men were talking or napping; Snake was puffing unmelodiously on his harmonica while the horses dozed, swishing lazily at flies.

Katie had been watching Billy Claude, who was squatting in the pine needles, running his hands over Diablo's slender forelegs.

"He reminds me of Chris," she said suddenly.

Cole, following her gaze, nodded. "Your son? Billy Claude's a good kid. Has a nice touch with animals."

"He's so gentle. He'd make a good vet."

"Well . . . I don't know if he'd ever go back to school. Did a good job with Diablo, though, I'll say that for him."

"With Diablo? I noticed the scars. What happened to him, Cole?"

Cole picked up a piece of yellow pine bark and pulled pieces of it off and dropped them to the ground between his feet. "Interesting history. Diablo used to be a rodeo horse. Bulldogging."

"Bulldogging?"

"Yeah—it's a rodeo event. Takes two men, two horses, working together as a team. One rider is the hazer. His job is to keep the bull, or steer, close in. Prevent him from veering off course. The other rider, the dogger, picks his moment, drops down onto the steer's neck, grabs him by the horns, twists his head around until he has no choice but to go down, flat out on his side." He grinned at Katie, who was staring at him in horror. "Piece o' cake. Don't worry—it's not as bad as it sounds. The ol' steer just gets up and trots away like nothing happened."

"And the . . . dogger?"

"If his time is any good, if his horse and the hazer and *his* horse have all done their jobs, he takes home a share of the prize money."

"Oh. So what happened—"

"To Diablo? He got gored." Katie winced, made a sound. Cole glanced at her. "It happens—not as often as you might think, but it does happen. He healed up okay, but after that he'd shy away from a steer now and then, so he couldn't be trusted as a part of that team anymore, you follow me? So then they tried to make a saddle bronc out of him. He wouldn't buck, but he went crazy in the chute—cut himself up pretty badly. I bought him at auction—cheap. Billy Claude's been working with him. He's turning out to be a pretty fair roping horse."

"He's comin' along good," Billy Claude said, joining them. "He doesn't shy at all anymore, Cole."

Cole smiled and went on pulling off pieces of bark. "Well now, Billy—"

"Hardly at all. He could haze again, Cole, if I worked him."

"Billy," Cole said, shaking his head, "don't trust that horse too far, too fast, you understand me? Don't want you gettin' hurt, now."

And Katie hadn't been able to take her eyes off Cole's face. Lean, tan, smile lines softening the eagle's glare. She was thinking, *He's so much more than I thought he was! How many layers are there to this man?*

Now, sitting in the Sunday solitude of her tent, she thought that he was like a puzzle, and she was trying to put him together. *Or take him apart.* She suddenly found herself remembering Cole's hands as they had idly toyed with that piece of yellow pine bark, pulling off the jigsaw pieces of it, one by one.

There was a darn good analogy there, she thought, if she could only figure out how to put it into words.

She was still sitting quietly, thinking about it while her felt-tip pen dried out and the coffee in her mug turned cold, when she heard the chopper. Her heartbeat quickened, timing itself to the rhythm of the rotors. Cole was back.

She told herself, I will not go running out to meet him. It would be silly.

But her legs were stiff and her coffee was cold. She could use a stretch anyway. And it would be just as silly to go out of her way to avoid him. Wouldn't it?

She took her time about it, standing up, stretching, patting her hair and tugging down her sweater, gathering up her sandwich plate and coffee mug. As an afterthought, removing her glasses and dropping them onto her sleeping bag. As she crossed the slope to the cookhouse she tried hard not to look down toward the meadow, but when movement caught the corner of her eye, the glance was reflexive. And then she dropped all pretense of indifference and just stood there, watching him stride up the hill toward her.

It was like watching the sun rise.

Cole checked his stride when he saw her, a reflex, like throwing up an arm to ward off a blow. It felt like a blow, what the sight of her did to him. Like a punch in the stomach.

It surprised him, really surprised him, the way he was reacting to seeing her there. She wasn't beautiful, not by the standards he was accustomed to. She was attractive, sure, with that magnificent hair catching the sun like that; a tall, slender redhead with a kind of natural elegance about her. But he knew he wasn't reacting to what she *looked* like, so much as who she *was*.

In a very short time, it seemed, K. T. Winslow had come to mean something to him. Something very special.

When he got closer to her she waved at him with a tin plate. Feeling like a high-school kid he smiled at her and said, "Hi, how ya doin'?"

She smiled back and said, "Okay. How was your trip?" Her voice seemed a bit husky. He wondered if she was catching a cold.

He shrugged. "It was okay. Had a few phone calls to make."

She hesitated, cleared her throat, said, "Well," and turned away, muttering something under her breath about coffee.

"Katherine."

She turned back. Her cheeks were pinker than usual. He wanted to touch them with his fingers.

"Katherine, I'm going to have to go back."

"Back?"

"Yeah. Back to the big city. Some things I've been putting off won't wait any longer, they tell me. Preproduction meetings, things like that. The real world calling."

She was nodding. "I understand. When?"

"Right now. This afternoon. Sandy's got the motor running, in fact."

"Oh." He saw her swallow. "How long will you be gone?"

"Won't be back. That's why I thought I'd better come back and get you. You see, I—"

"Get me?"

"Yeah, the work here's about to wind up anyway. Everybody'll be moving back down to the ranch in a few days, so you might just as well come with me now on the chopper, while you've got the chance. Besides—"

"The chopper?"

"Sure." Cole grinned at her. "Beats a long trek on old Jackson, any day."

"But I really don't *mind*—"

"Besides." He felt his smile slip sideways. "You need to see what Cole Grayson's like in real life anyway. Can't hardly get to know me without that, can you?" He felt the cold edges of his shell creeping around him. His smile began to feel like a mask. He barely noticed that she was staring at him with something like horror.

"No, Cole, you don't understand. I can't—"

But what it was she couldn't do she never got a chance to tell him. Just then Frankie came tearing up the hill on that paint mare of his, both of them in a lather. Frankie was yelling, "Cole! Come on, man, it's Billy Claude! Diablo threw him. He's hurt, man. I think it's bad!"

Eight

"Come on, we'll take the chopper." Cole grabbed Katherine's hand, sending both the plate and mug flying. She hauled back on his arm like a balky mule.

"No, wait, Cole. I can't."

"Dammit, Katherine, come on! I might need you."

Frankie was yelling at him to get the first-aid kit. He shouted back, "There's one in the chopper. Katherine . . ."

She gave a helpless-sounding whimper and moved.

On the way down the hill Cole asked Frankie, "Okay, you want to tell me what in the hell happened? Where'd you leave him? How bad is he hurt?"

"He's down in Blue Meadow. I left—"

"What the hell were you doing in Blue Meadow? What the hell were you doing with Diablo—" He stopped, and Katherine ran right into him. He noticed that her eyes seemed a little glassy, and she was pale, too. Maybe she *was* coming down with something, but he couldn't think about that just then. "You guys were doggin' steers, weren't you?" He was mad enough to jerk Frankie right out of his saddle. "Damn fool kid! I told him—I just got through telling him—not to try it with that horse yet!" He *was* mad enough to yank Frankie out of his saddle, and did. He held him by the collar and shook him a couple of times. "He wasn't gored, was he? You didn't leave him out there bleeding—"

"No! No, man—it wasn't like that. Diablo shied and threw him, and the steer ran right over him. Trampled him, maybe kicked him in the head, hell, I don't know! Look, man—it wasn't even my idea!"

"Yeah . . . look, I'm sorry." Cole could see the kid was upset, scared. He slapped him on the back and gave his shoulder a squeeze. "Hey, good thing the chopper's right here. We'll take care of him. No point in your coming—we'll have him picked up before you even get there. Go on back. Tell Birdie what's happened. Get yourself something to drink. And don't worry, okay? He'll be all right."

Cole wasn't sure he believed that himself, but Frankie seemed to. He swallowed a couple of times, said "Yeah . . . yeah, okay," and got back on his horse. Cole took Katherine's hand and went on down the hill. Her hand felt cold as ice. Well, he thought, it was understandable she'd be pretty upset. She'd had kind of a special thing going with Billy Claude. Probably because the kid reminded her of her own son. Probably she was seeing her own kid lying hurt right this minute. It would explain why she looked so pale.

Darn kid. Cole stared resolutely through the chopper's bubble, straining to see beyond the trees to Blue Meadow. *Darn fool kid.*

He saw Diablo first, standing head down in the grass, placidly grazing, oblivious to the still form sprawled near his feet. He nudged Sandy's arm and pointed. Sandy nodded and set the chopper neatly down in a swirl of dry meadow grass and bugs.

Cole yelled, "Katherine—bring the first-aid kit!" and hit the ground running.

Billy Claude was awake, but in pain. There was blood

on his face. He looked white and scared. He said "Cole—" in a thin, raspy voice, and coughed. The cough made his face crumple and go gray. ". . . Hurts, Cole."

"I know," Cole said gently, smoothing lank strands of yellow hair back from the boy's forehead. It felt clammy. The kid was probably in shock, on top of everything else. "Can you tell me where?"

"Hurts . . . when I breathe. Damn steer . . . stepped right in the middle of me. . . ."

"Okay, kid, you're gonna be fine. Just hang on, all right? Take it easy." He looked back at the chopper. What in the hell was keeping Katherine? He needed that first-aid kit. He needed a blanket, a stretcher. Dammit, where was she? He couldn't see her anywhere!

Sandy came running, carrying a wool blanket and the emergency kit. "How is he?"

Cole stood up and went to meet him. "Not great. Broken ribs, for sure; maybe some internal injuries. Got anything we can use for a stretcher? Where's Katherine, anyway?"

"Over there," Sandy said, jerking his head toward the chopper. "Around behind. Bein' sick, I think."

Cole swore.

"Scared to death of flyin'," Sandy said with a grunt, squatting on his heels to spread the blanket over Billy Claude. "Don't know how you even got her into that chopper."

Cole swore some more. Unaccustomed emotions boiled and seethed inside him—anger, tenderness, and fear all mixed up together, for both her and Billy Claude. He took two steps toward the chopper, then two steps back. And then, since Sandy looked as if he knew what he was doing, threw up his hands and ran for the chopper.

He found Katherine sitting in the grass under the swishing rotors, with her head resting on her pulled-up knees. He stopped, took a deep breath, hesitated, then put his hand on the back of her neck and gently squeezed.

"I'm sorry," she said in a small voice. "You didn't need this."

"It's okay. Why didn't you tell me?"

"I sort of tried. It didn't seem like the time. I don't know. How is he?"

"Not good. Broken ribs, maybe internal injuries, and I don't know what else. At least we've got the chopper right here. We'll get him to the hospital in Bishop. He'll be okay." At least he hoped so.

"I'm sorry," Katherine said again. "Go on—take care of Billy. I'll be fine."

He saw that she would be, so he left her and went back to help Sandy. Between the two of them, using the blanket for a stretcher, they managed to get Billy Claude into the chopper without doing too much further damage. But that left room for only one more passenger.

Standing in the rotor's turbulence while Sandy revved up for takeoff, Cole hesitated, looking at Katherine. She wasn't so pale now, at least. He glanced over at Diablo and back at her. The wind whipped long strands of her hair loose and drew them across her face. She reached up to pull them away, holding onto him with her eyes the way a drowning man hangs onto a tree limb.

Raising his voice above the racket of the chopper he said, "I've got to go with him."

She nodded. He could see her lips move to form, "I know," though he couldn't hear her say it.

"Can you take Diablo back to camp?"

She just nodded, looking and looking at him. For a few seconds he looked back at her while the rotors whipped overhead. Then he stepped forward and put his arms around her. He held her close but not hard, wrapping her up in his arms as if she were something precious he needed to shield and protect, while inside him something swelled and grew until he thought he'd burst. Before that could happen, he tipped her chin up, kissed her forehead, stepped back, and hauled himself into the chopper. He gave Sandy a thumbs-up signal, and the ground dropped away. When he looked back, Katherine was still standing there holding her hair in one hand, shielding her eyes with the other. He watched her until he couldn't see her any more, and then turned to speak encouraging words to Billy Claude.

Katie waited until the helicopter was only a speck in the blue sky, disappearing beyond the pine trees, then went over to Diablo and picked up the dangling ends of his reins. Billy Claude's hat was lying there on the ground. She picked it up and dusted it against her pant leg. Then she put her arms around Diablo's neck, pressed her face into the warm hide, and burst into tears. She wasn't sure exactly why she was crying, but it felt good, so she went ahead and did it until she didn't feel like doing it any more. When she had run out of tears she brushed her cheeks with her hands, took a deep breath, and climbed onto Diablo's back.

Diablo was a lamb, and after Jackson's bone-jarring gait, riding him was like sitting in a rocking chair. Nevertheless, Katie rode all the way to camp at a sedate walk, and was glad to turn the big black animal over to Frankie.

Birdie brought her a big glass of lemonade and wanted to hear all about Billy Claude's condition. Katie told her everything she knew, which wasn't much, and then Frankie came back from the corrals and wanted to know how Billy Claude was, so she had to tell it all over again. By the time she'd finished, the men were beginning to straggle back from Monache, and the story had to be repeated for every new arrival.

After that, everybody just sat around the cookhouse, drinking coffee and lemonade and talking, the men all trying to outdo one another telling stories of horrible accidents and gruesome injuries. Katie sat and listened to them. Her eyes felt hot and sticky—from her fit of weeping, she supposed—but she didn't want to go back to her tent and lie down.

It was nearly suppertime when they finally heard the chopper. Everybody got up and sort of ambled out of the cookhouse to wait for Cole, nobody wanting to show how worried he was by walking down to meet him, but everybody wanting to see right away by his face that Billy Claude was going to be okay.

And he was. Cole looked tired, but he was smiling. "Broken ribs," he said, finding Katie in the crowd of men. "Slight concussion, shock. I guess the shock was the worst thing, but they've got him stabilized, and they say he's going to be fine. They don't think there are any internal injuries, but they'll run a few more tests, just to make sure. He'll be sore for a while, but he'll be okay."

There was a kind of collective release of breath, an easing of indefinable tension. Like a knot unraveling, the men dispersed, talking and laughing, and Birdie went back to grumbling and banging pots around in the shed. Cole took Katie by the arm and walked with her a little way down the slope, then turned toward her. His gaze was the eagle's again—piercing and golden. It turned her bones to sawdust.

"Well, how did you get along with Diablo?" His voice was soft, in contrast to the look in his eyes.

Katie had to cough a little before she could reply, "Fine. He's easier to ride than Jackson, actually."

"Want to ride him home?"

She frowned in bewilderment. "Home?"

"I still have to be in L.A. by Monday afternoon."

She opened her mouth to ask about the chopper, then closed it again as the eggbeater sound of it came clearly, fading away into the distance.

Cole put his hands on her shoulders, then moved them together behind her neck, under her hair. His smile made her stop breathing. Her stomach hurt.

"That's something else I'm going to have to break you of, you know that? This unreasonable fear you have. I guess I'll have to show you the *sensual* joys of flying."

"The *what* of flying? Cole—"

"But not today. Enough is enough for one day. I sent Sandy back to the ranch and told him to have Rob meet us at the river with a truck for the horses. If we leave right now and push it, we should be able to make it by dark."

"By dark? Cole, it took Snake and me almost all day—"

"Yeah, but that was a week ago, and you were stuck with ol' Jackson, remember? That was before I taught you how to *ride.* You've come a long way, baby."

Katie gazed at him and thought, Yes, she certainly had.

One week ago she'd come to the high country to meet a reclusive movie star. She'd been a tenderfoot on a jugheaded nag, a city girl moaning about the sun, the heat, the dirt, the bugs, too vain to face a bunch of cowboys with dirt on her face. In one week, with Cole's help, she'd discovered the beauty of the wild country; the bunch of cowboys had become *people*, each one interesting and unique in his way; she'd ridden bareback at dawn, with the wind in her hair; and for the first time in her life she'd fallen deeply, genuinely, wonderfully, ridiculously in love—with the movie star!

She'd come a very long way. So far, she was afraid she'd never find her way back to the place she'd been before.

"Um," she said, holding her hair close to her head as if that might help to keep herself together. "What about my things?"

Cole snapped his fingers. "Damn! I knew I was forgetting something. Should have had Sandy take 'em. Oh, well—just leave everything here for now. I'll have it picked up later when we break camp."

"But—"

"Just bring your personal things, a change of clothes—whatever you can fit in saddlebags. Hurry up—I'll go see if Birdie can fix us something to eat on the way. Meet me up at the corrals in . . . ten minutes."

She really had lost it, she thought, staring after him. She had completely lost control of her life.

"Well, that's that," Cole said, giving Diablo's rump a slap that sent the big black trotting into the corral, head down to sniff the unfamiliar turf. "Wonder what's keeping the truck?" It was the third time he'd said that since they'd arrived at the river crossing at dusk to find the camp deserted, and that wasn't like him.

Sure, he was worried—both Sandy and Rob were reliable, so for the truck to be this late there had to be a problem of some kind. He and Katherine were pretty well stranded—it was a long way to the ranch from this base camp, and the horses were tired. But his uneasiness was more than that. More, even, than the usual edginess that came over him when he knew he was going to have to go back to L.A. for an indefinite period of time. Right now he felt as jumpy as a teenager, and he knew exactly what was causing it. . . .

It was a summer night. The air felt soft on the skin and smelled of the river, a rich, brown smell, evocative of more carefree days. There was a three-quarter moon washing the land with silver and indigo. And there was Katherine.

He didn't have to touch her to feel her with every nerve in his body. Just now she was stretching, rubbing her back and rotating her head. He reached toward her, wanting to put his hands on her shoulders, wanting to help ease the stiffness with gentle massage, but drew back before he could touch her. It would be dangerous, touching her now. . . .

"Tired?" he asked softly.

"Yeah, a little. What I'd really love is a *bath*." He heard her low laughter. "Story of my life."

Smiling, he said, "Well, there's a river over there."

"Thanks, but I think I've learned my lesson. I'll wait. I've been dreaming of a nice hot shower for about the last two hours."

"Can't figure what's keeping the truck," Cole said once more. "Well, no telling how long we'll be waiting. I guess we might just as well make ourselves comfortable." He untied the rolled blanket he always carried on his saddle, hefted Katherine's saddlebags, and touched her elbow. "Come on—there's a good place over here."

He spread the blanket on a large, flat rock overlooking the river, and dropped the saddlebags onto it. "This used to be our picnic rock when I was a kid. There was a rope right over there—you could swing out over the water and drop in. There was a nice deep pool there where that sandbar is now."

"It looks like there's a deep spot right below this rock," Katherine said, walking to the edge and peering down. "I'll bet you could dive from here."

"That's a good way to wind up dead from the neck down," Cole said, sitting down on the blanket with a groan. He took off his hat and let it dangle between his drawn-up knees while the night air dried the sweat on his forehead. As if unable to stay away, his gaze came to rest on Katherine, now just a dark silhouette against the silvery ripple of moonlit water. She was still standing, reluctant to share his blanket, tense and edgy as he was. He thought he knew why she felt uncomfortable with him—without actually putting it in words, she'd offered him love, and he'd rejected it.

Love. In his world it was a commodity, and cheap, at that.

He sat watching the river roll silently by, thinking about love, and Katherine. He supposed it could be love, what he felt for her—it was very different from the way he'd felt about Mia, but that had been a long time ago, and he was a different person now, too. He watched the water and thought that people's lives were a lot like moving streams. He thought about clichés like "water under the bridge."

But streams come together, too, he thought suddenly; they merge to make larger streams. And sometimes the coming together of two streams isn't easy. The merging causes undercurrents, turbulence, white water—

"You're very quiet," Katherine said. Her voice was breathy, with its own undercurrents.

"Katherine," he said harshly, surprising himself because he'd promised himself he'd never ask her this, "tell me about your divorce."

Katie heard the rasp in his voice, and it surprised her more than the question. She wondered, as she had that afternoon at the hot springs, what powerful emotions, what secret, painful memories, put it there.

"Oh," she said on a rueful little laugh, "there isn't much to tell. It was . . . your basic divorce, no more or less painful than any, I guess."

"Bull. It left you scarred."

She stared at his form in the darkness and didn't reply. After a moment he said softly, "Tell me, Katherine. I really want to know."

As if, she thought, he really *needed* to know.

There had been a time when she'd done almost nothing but talk about it—the anguish, the fear, the guilt. But that had been a long time ago, and she was a different person now. Now, remembering what had been the very worst time of her life, she felt only a faint ache of regret.

She sat down on the blanket beside Cole, facing the river, as he did, arms hugging her drawn-up legs. "It was a classic case of marrying too young and for the wrong reasons, I suppose. I was in high school—I told you what I looked like."

"What you *felt* you looked like."

"That's what counts, Cole. Anyway, David was older, and in the army, and I really thought it made me something special, to be dating a serviceman. A uniform—wow. I was flattered that he seemed to . . . desire me. And thrilled to death when he asked me to marry him. What I didn't realize then was how inse-cure *he* was. He needed someone like me to feel supe-rior to, someone he could control."

"How long did it take you to come to your senses?" Cole's voice had a sharp edge.

"It was a gradual thing, my growing up, and it took a lot longer than it might have, because we moved around so much, and I was so dependent on him for . . . everything. Emotional nourishment, I learned to call it later. But eventually, inevitably, I did grow up, and he didn't like me grown up. He needed a little girl to look up to him, I guess. So he began to reject me in every way possible. I felt worthless and unattractive. It took me years to realize that I could take control of my life and change things."

"Katherine, how long were you married?"

Her reply was as soft as the question. "Sixteen years."

Cole's silence was eloquent. After a while he asked, "Your career—was that cause or effect?"

"Both, I guess. I told you, I had always had great fantasies. And I had always put them down on paper—it was therapy, I think. Escapism. And then I discovered that other people needed to escape as much as I did, and that there was a market for fantasy. Success fed my self-esteem. What happened became . . . inevitable."

"Inevitable . . . but not easy."

"Oh, no." This time her laugh carried remembered pain. "Sundering relationships is never easy."

"No," Cole said. He cleared his throat and was silent.

He knows that, too, Katie thought. She wanted so badly to ask him how he knew; in a way, it was her job to ask. She sensed that he would tell her, that he *wanted* to tell her, but that he would choose his own time and place.

So she let the silence fill up with the sounds of the river and the summer night—frogs and insects and night birds and the soft whickering of the horses in the corrals—and after a while she stirred restlessly and murmured, "I sure wish that truck would hurry up. I really do need a shower. I *itch.*"

He chuckled. "I know what you mean." His voice sounded more like the Cole she knew—intimate, relaxed, carrying traces of a drawl.

"And I reek of horses and sweat. Hey," she said, warming to the change of subject. "That reminds me of something. I've always wondered about that movie, the one with what's-her-name, where you and the spoiled banker's daughter are running from the bad guys through the badlands of Texas, or someplace—"

"Sara Fielding," Cole said, a smile in his voice. *"Rio Grande."*

"Right. You know what I kept thinking about? How hot it was, and how long those two—you two—had been wearing the same clothes, without bathing."

"Katherine, you are a true romantic!"

"Well, I have to tell you, it did kind of spoil the love scenes for me."

Cole was laughing. "Actually, you hit pretty close to the truth. We were on location in Utah for three weeks, filming that movie. It was hotter than hell, and if you think my cow camp is primitive—at least there you have a creek! During the filming, water had to be trucked in for the whole crew. So the dirt and sweat were pretty real."

"Well," Katie said with a sniff, "it didn't do the romance any good, I'll tell you that. All I can ever think about in situations like that is, how on earth do they stand each other!"

"Actually," Cole said, still chuckling, "it's probably like eating onions—if everybody's in the same boat, nobody minds it. Do you mean to tell me your characters never get dirty?"

"Oh, sure they do—but they also *bathe.* A *lot.*"

"I see. So . . . bathing is romantic." His voice was heavy with amusement—and something else. Katie could tell that he had turned his head and was looking at her in the dark. She could almost see the soft, golden light in his eyes, the laugh lines at the corners of his mouth. Around them the air began to take on texture and substance.

"Well," Katie murmured, "some kinds of bathing certainly are. I can't say much for ice water."

"Oh, I don't know. It had its moments."

In his voice was the timbre of intimate knowledge. Katie said huskily, "Cole. You *were* peeking!"

"Did you really expect me not to? Geez, woman, I'm only human. I keep trying to tell you that."

They were both laughing, sharing the laughter and a strange, quivery excitement. Katie felt as if her teeth would chatter if she didn't keep her jaws tensed. Her breathing felt shallow and uneven. "Cole," she said after a moment, "what are you doing?"

"Taking my boots off."

"You're not—"

"Yes, I am. This conversation has got me to feeling like I can't stand myself right now. No telling how long it'll be before we're rescued, and a skinny-dip in the moonlight seems like as good a way as any to pass the time."

"Skinny-dip?" Katie said faintly.

"Well, unless you'd rather go in in your clothes. Personally—"

"You're not serious."

"Sure, I am. I'm itchy too. Are you coming? Might just as well, since I've already seen what you look like."

Katie gasped. "You *are* serious." And yet "serious" seemed a long way from describing the mood that had come over them. Maybe it was the culmination of a long, emotionally intense day; maybe they were so tired, they weren't thinking clearly. Maybe it was moon madness. They were giddy, but there was an odd kind of recklessness in the silliness, too, a kind of "ah, the hell with it!" attitude. There was a fantasy feel to what was happening; they felt as if it didn't really matter what they did or said, because it wasn't real anyway.

Cole stood up to unbutton his shirt, then his Levis.

He had to hop on one foot to get his pants off, which made Katie giggle. She felt drunk. The moonlight turned his body to silver, lent it a weird, alien beauty. She wondered if it would make her body look like that too. . . .

Cole slipped out of sight over the edge of the rock. Katie heard him swear softly under his breath, and then there was a change in the sound of the river as it altered its course around the new obstruction.

"Ah! Cold, but feels great! Are you coming?"

Katie peered down at the water and wondered if she dared go in. She wasn't ashamed of her body—she took care to stay in shape, and knew she looked better than most people her age and even those a lot younger. Besides, it was dark . . . sort of. He couldn't really see her, and even if he could, so what? So what? . . . The fog of giddiness thinned slightly, letting in a glimmer of common sense.

Just then, like a cartoon devil prodding her with his pitchfork, something began to itch tenaciously between her shoulder blades, just where she couldn't reach it. A mosquito sang near her ear.

"All right," she said breathlessly, "I'm coming in. Close your eyes."

Cole's reply to that absurdity was an eloquent snort. After a moment he said, "Katherine, you're not really going to leave your underwear on, are you?"

"Look, I'm sorry. I can't help it. I'm a product of my era."

"Don't you know that those two strips of white nylon make you a lot easier to see in the dark than if you were totally nude? And a lot sexier, too."

Katie gave a helpless whimper and lowered herself over the edge of the rock into the dark water. *There.* She'd done it. No going back now.

Nine

The water was cold. Not numbingly cold like the creek, but refreshing . . . exhilarating.

The river was wide and shallow, surrounded by river-bottom scrub and granite mountains and canopied by an indigo sky set with diamond stars and a sapphire moon. The water rippled in their light like black silk. The play of light and water on Cole's body made it shimmer, so that he seemed more like a mythical creature than a man. As he moved toward her through the waist-deep river she felt like a sprite in the thrall of a pagan god. . . .

They could have been alone in the universe. Katie knew that a midsummer river bottom must be a noisy place at night, but in the focused tension around them there was silence. Neither of them broke it with unnecessary words. Cole held out his hand and she placed hers into it. The sandy riverbed dropped gently away under her feet as he led her into deeper water.

When the water reached the tops of her breasts he turned her to face him and let go of her hand. She could see the pale gleam of his smile. They floated there, not touching, not speaking, yet in a strange sort of intimacy more profound than a shared shower. Water covered her to her chest, yet she'd never felt so naked; when she began to wash herself, letting her hands glide slowly over her body's curves and hollows, she felt that his eyes followed them, touching wherever they touched.

Presently, so quietly, it didn't disturb the rhythms of the night, Cole said, "Feels good, doesn't it?"

Katie whispered, "Yes."

"Still itch?"

"No, except between my shoulder blades. I can't seem to reach it."

"Here, let me."

Obediently Katie turned her back and moved away from him, back into shallower water, where it was easier to brace against the current. The river made small musical sounds to mark her movements and Cole's. A moment later she felt his hand on her shoulder, and then a delicious abrasion on her back.

"Umm . . . that's wonderful. What is it?"

"Sand. Katherine . . ." She felt his hand move on her shoulder, following the line of her bra strap. "Do you think we could get rid of this foolishness now?"

"Yes," she whispered. And then, "It fastens in front." She held her breath. The water slipped past her waist in a long, cool caress. Underfoot the sand moved and shifted, making her feel precarious, unbalanced. Somehow she seemed to be leaning . . . leaning toward the hard, solid form at her back.

Cole's thumb stroked slowly along the ridge of her collarbone, then slipped downward. Katie brought her water-chilled hand up to meet his in the hollow between her breasts. There was a barely audible click, and the clammy touch of nylon was replaced by an enveloping warmth that seemed to penetrate deep, deep inside her. She drew in her breath in a long sigh, lifting her chest, pushing against his hand in a gentle and entirely natural way.

With his other hand he rubbed her back in delicate circles, gently chafing her skin with the sand, sensitizing it, awakening every nerve, moving slowly down, down, until the water took away the sand and there was nothing but his hand gliding over the cold-roughened swell of her bottom.

She whispered, "Cole . . ."

His reply was a low sound of affirmation. His head descended; for just a moment she felt the rasp of his jaw against the side of her face, his breath in the shell of her ear. His mouth touched below her ear and moved, hot and open, along the taut cord of her neck. Shudders racked her. Her skin was so cold, his mouth so hot. She burned with cold, prickly fires, as if all the sparklers from every Fourth of July she'd ever known had ignited just under her skin.

Cold on the outside . . . skin rough with it, nipples hard and aching . . . Hot inside . . . not searing heat, but something heavy and liquid that felt like melting. She'd forgotten that hot-cold feeling! Forgotten the way it pulsed in every vein, shivered through every nerve. Forgotten that it had the power to buckle her knees and make her gasp and whimper with wanting.

Cole's hand slid around inside her panties, smoothed the sharp edge of her pelvis, and splayed across her belly. He drew her close, holding her just like that, with one arm angling across her aching breasts, the other pressed hard against the lower part of her body. He held her very still, letting her feel the heat in his body, letting her know the rhythm of his heartbeat. She turned her head, searching for his mouth, losing herself in it. Rhythms slowed, became torpid and heavy. His hand moved lower, housing the center of her body in warmth while his fingers slipped between her thighs. Standing there in the chilly water, caught between his hand and his body, she was enveloped in heat; when her own body ignited, she could only gasp and writhe closer to him, seeking the fire's source.

Around them, the night filled with noise.

Cole lifted his head. Katie asked thickly, "Is that thunder?"

"It's the truck," Cole said.

They stood motionless together, listening. Katie made a little sound of frustration. "It's coming up the grade," Cole muttered. "Be here in five minutes or so. Don't panic."

"I'm not panicking," Katie said. "Just suicidal."

"Well," Cole said, "it's probably just as well."

Katie's body gave a little involuntary jerk, and Cole's arms tightened around her. She felt tension tremors chase each other through his muscles, and his voice was a harsh growl in her ear.

"Dammit, Katherine, it's not because I don't want to make love to you! You know damn well I do. And if the truck hadn't come, I sure as hell would have, and hated myself in the morning for it."

She jerked again, and again he refused to let her pull away from him. "Why?" she asked huskily. "You wouldn't have exactly seduced a virgin, you know."

He sighed, and rubbed her temple with his chin. "Yeah, in a way I would. Katherine, you don't know me. You don't have any idea who you're dealing with, who I really am. *Hush!*" he said when she would have interrupted him. His voice was guttural, strained. "You think I'm some kind of hero—yes, you do—and I'm not. *Believe* me I'm not! You're going to find that out pretty soon, and when you do . . ." He turned her gently in his arms, and touched her chin with his fist, making her look at him. "When you do, if you still feel like making love with me, let me know."

He lowered his head and kissed her, a sensual, lingering caress that made a sharp little pain go corkscrewing through her chest. "I'll put on my pants and go stall the truck. Take your time."

"Where's my bra?" Katie asked hoarsely. It was all she could do to talk at all. Her jaws felt cramped; she was overwhelmed with unreasoning anger and frustration, but too vulnerable to argue.

"About five miles down the river, I'd say. It's gonna make some lucky trout fisherman's day."

Everything she was feeling—the helplessness, the rage, the pain—she heard echoed in the unfamiliar pitch of Cole's laughter.

" 'Mornin', sunshine. Come on, let's go!"

Katie groaned. Recurring nightmare, part two. At least, she thought, levering one eye open, it really did seem to be morning this time. She glared at Cole's clean-shaven face through her one functional eye, muttered "Go 'way," and pulled the covers over her head.

"Not at our best in the morning, are we?" Cole said cheerfully, heartlessly peeling the blankets away from her face. "Sorry to have to do this to you, but I have a noon meeting in L.A. Rob should be here in about"—he glanced at his watch—"half an hour, to take us to the plane."

The plane. Cole was taking her to Los Angeles in his airplane. How could she have forgotten something like that? Even with everything that had happened the night before . . .

She cleared her throat, then glanced hurriedly down at herself to see what she was wearing. A T-shirt, thank God—one of Cole's, probably. She sat up carefully.

"Katherine," he said softly, "you okay?"

"Yes," she said. "I'm fine."

"I mean about the flying."

"I said I'm *fine*. I'll be okay. Just go away and let me get dressed." She rubbed her hand over her eyes, keeping them closed so she wouldn't have to meet his. She knew that right now Cole's eyes, with their warm amber glow and radiating smile lines, would be more than she could handle.

With relief she felt his weight leave the edge of the bed. From a greater distance she heard him murmur, "Coffee's hot. I'll see you in the kitchen, then." She heard his boots on the hardwood floor, and the sound of the door closing behind him.

I'm fine. She lay back on the pillows and put her arm over her eyes. *I'll be okay.* She'd said that to herself a lot, in the last years of her marriage and through the traumatic months of separation and divorce. It had been a long time since she'd felt shaky enough to need to give herself a pep talk.

It had been a graveyard hour of the morning by the time she'd finally dragged herself into bed, aching in both body and spirit. The truck's tardiness had turned out to be due to a flat tire. Cole's brother, Rob, had changed the tire by himself on the narrow mountain grade, only to discover that the spare was flat as well. He'd had to hike for miles back to the main highway to flag down a passing car to take him to a telephone, then wait for someone from the ranch to come and bring him another tire! Poor Rob.

But at least, Katie thought, his problems had solutions.

Oh, Katie, she thought, how could you have let yourself get into a situation like this? How could you be so *dumb?*

Right now she ached all over, mostly inside. She vibrated with excess energy, like a race car in neutral. She wanted to run away to someplace where nobody knew her name, and hide. Katie knew the symptoms all too well. *She was scared.* Not of the flying—that was a finite fear, something she could manage, if she had to. This was something much worse, something she'd become very familiar with after making the decision to end her marriage. It was fear of the unknown, fear of the future, fear of *life.* She couldn't see how this was going to turn out, couldn't see how she could possibly avoid getting hurt.

134 · KATHLEEN CREIGHTON

And she should have known better! A person couldn't very well get involved with a mega-star without expecting to get hurt. To allow herself to fall in love with one was just plain stupid.

But she'd be fine. She'd be okay. She'd survived much worse than this. It was just that, at forty falling in love for real, for the first time, was . . . well, a bit disconcerting. Once she got some perspective on this thing she'd be okay. As soon as she got back to L.A. she'd call the kids and have a good talk. She'd call Sonya, her agent, and they'd have lunch and talk about editors and royalties and book contracts . . . important things. To hell with love! All she needed was some serious shopping!

Shopping. All she had to her name, at the moment, was a change of underwear, a clean shirt, and yesterday's dirty Levis!

She'd spent some time soaking the saddle weariness out of her bones last night, so it didn't take her long to wash her face, brush her teeth, and twist her hair into a loose coil. Amazing, she thought as she went through the vital ritual of making up her face, how rosy and fit she looked, considering the way she felt. All that wholesome air and Birdie's cooking must have agreed with her.

She didn't have time for coffee, which was probably just as well—she was wired enough. By the time she'd finished in the bathroom, Rob was waiting at the front gate in a Jeep, and Cole was pounding on the door, yelling, "Come on, Katherine, hurry up! You can do that when we get there!"

Katie wondered briefly just exactly where "there" was, as she grabbed up the saddlebags containing her personal belongings, took a last, sustaining breath, and opened the door.

Last night in the darkness she hadn't been able to get much of an idea what Cole's ranch was like. Now she saw that in its own way it was as serene and isolated as his Sierra cow camp, and as far removed from life's fast lane. His brother, Rob, was a slender, quiet man, with thinning hair and nut-brown skin. He drove the Jeep down long, shaded lanes between rows of huge, gnarled cottonwoods, giving Katie glimpses of neat, old-fashioned clapboard houses, picket fences, rambling roses and hollyhocks, bunkhouses and corral fences, great wooden barns and concrete silos. Then they were driving under a hot morning sun and cloudless cobalt sky, through seemingly endless fields of oats and alfalfa, and the air was filled with the scent of hay and the sound of sprinklers.

The plane looked remarkably pretty, sitting there on the white runway in the middle of emerald-green fields. Katie sat staring at it through the Jeep's bug-spattered windshield while Cole took her saddlebags from her nerveless hands and stowed them in the plane. It was red and white, and very clean, like a brand-new toy.

"All set?" he asked, smiling kindly at her.

She nodded, swallowed acid, and held out her hand. As she climbed stiffly out of the Jeep, Rob Grayson reached out to give her hand a reassuring squeeze that made Katie wonder what Cole had told him about her. Then he put the Jeep in gear and went rocketing off in a cloud of dust.

Cole put his arm around Katie's waist and walked her to the plane. "Katherine," he said softly, "I'm not going to try to convince you with reason that there's nothing to fear. It wouldn't work, because your fear isn't rational. You have to overcome it with faith."

"Faith?" She felt cold, even in the August heat.

"Yeah, faith." He turned her to face him and touched her chin with his fist, making her meet his eyes. They were a deep, rich amber, full of things she couldn't fathom, but that made her want to fall in and drown. "Katherine, you'll just have to trust me."

"Trust you?"

"Do you?"

She licked her lips. "Yes."

"All right, then. Up you go."

He helped her into the plane and fastened her securely into the passenger's seat, then got out and walked around carefully checking everything before finally releasing the cables that tethered them to the ground. He climbed into the pilot's seat, fastened his shoulder harness, and gave her a smile and a thumbs-up signal. And then, before she even knew what was happening, they were speeding down the runway, with green fields and sprinklers flashing by on either side. The wheels vibrated on the rough earth, and then abruptly the vibrating stopped and Katie felt herself grow heavy in her seat. She shut her eyes tightly and pressed her lips together on a whimper as her ears recorded the altitude change. There was a horrifying sensation of weightlessness, and she gripped the seat, bracing herself for oblivion. The plane banked to the left and encountered a bit of thermal turbulence. Katie felt herself break into a cold sweat; nausea clutched at her throat. And then all at once they were cruising, with only the guttural drone of the engines to disturb the stillness.

"Katherine, open your eyes."

She did, and tried to smile.

"Feeling sick?"

She nodded.

"Nothin' to be ashamed of. Just put your head back and relax for a few minutes. It'll pass."

His voice was so calm and unconcerned. So reassuring. Katie did as he told her and presently the nausea did pass, and she began to feel peaceful. She watched Cole's strong brown hands on the controls of the frail little toy airplane and thought in quiet amazement, I really *do* trust him. It was a strange feeling for her, and strangely wonderful. She trusted Cole. He made her feel safe. And she suddenly realized that, for all her denial of it, and his, he really was a hero to her.

In a way, she'd come full circle. She'd gone from

thinking of Cole Grayson as a celluloid hero, a fantasy figure, bigger than life, to the realization that he was a living, breathing human being, a man capable of the whole spectrum of human frailty and emotion. Now she'd come back to thinking of him as a hero—but with a difference. Now he was *her* hero. And that, she felt with absolute certainty, was *right*. A man *should* be a hero to the woman who loves him.

A memory came to her, vivid, but painted in the misty pastel colors of nostalgia. Her grandfather, white-haired but still handsome, age-spotted hands steady on the steering wheel of his middle-aged Ford; her grandmother, sitting in the back seat placidly knitting as her husband threaded his way through heavy, rainy-day traffic. Her mother, tense and white-knuckled, saying with exasperation in her voice, "Mother, how can you just sit there knitting?" And her grandmother's reply in mild surprise: "Why, darling, I trust your father's driving." Katie remembered the look in her grandmother's eyes as she lifted them to rest, for one brief moment, on the back of her husband's neck. She'd seen the glow of love, and something more. *Hero worship.*

Quaintly old-fashioned . . . impossibly idealistic and unrealistic . . . maybe. But her grandparents were married to each other for sixty-two years and died within a year of each other, in the home they'd made together as newlyweds.

The plane's engines droned on. The pale buff of the desert slid slowly away beneath them and gave way to the blue ridges of the Angeles National Forest.

Cole glanced over at her and smiled. His smile made a warm pool inside her, like a cup of hot cocoa on a cold day. "Look," he said, pointing. "That's probably the only cloud in California today." It looked like a cotton ball, snagged on the jagged mountaintop. "Let's go see," Cole added, grinning at her as he banked the plane slightly.

As they approached it, the cloud began to look thinner, wispier. Then it stopped looking like a cloud at all and became fog. "Smell that," Cole said, drawing the moist air deep into his lungs. Katie closed her eyes and felt the cool kiss of it on her face. The breath she took wasn't quite steady; it brought inside her a new and fragile happiness.

The cloud dropped away behind them and was replaced by the brownish haze of the Los Angeles Basin. Cole was talking on the radio, making contact with the control tower at Santa Monica's municipal airport while they descended through the smog blanket. Katie swallowed to relieve the pressure on her eardrums, and unconsciously braced her feet. Then they touched lightly down, with barely a bump, and there was once again the sensation of speed as the ground rushed by in a gray blur.

A pewter-colored limousine was waiting for them at the gate. The chauffeur grinned when he saw them approaching, and took a cigar out of his pocket. Cole laughed and held out his hand.

"Sonofagun, Fergie. Tell me the good news, man!"

"A boy, what else? Daniel Cole Ferguson. Eight pounds, four ounces."

"Hey," Cole said, "that's great. How's Julie?"

"She's fine, just fine."

"Well, give her my love. Congratulations, both of you." Cole shook the man's hand warmly and pocketed the cigar. "Hey, Fergie, I'd like you to meet Katherine Winslow. Katherine, this is Kyle Ferguson. He used to be a stunt driver, but don't let that scare you. I'd trust this man with my life. Fact is, I guess I do, don't I?"

They all laughed.

Fergie held the door while Cole handed her into the car's plush, air-conditioned interior, then settled himself across from her.

"Care for a drink?"

Katie shook her head. The limousine began to move,

rolling silently and anonymously through familiar streets and onto the Santa Monica Freeway. As they headed east, toward downtown Los Angeles, Cole leaned forward and asked, "Well, Katherine, how'd you like the flight?"

Katie lifted her shoulders and smiled. Cole smiled back, a ghost of his old, intimate look. "Wasn't so bad after all, was it?"

"No," Katie whispered, but he'd already turned to gaze out the window, and she didn't think he'd even heard her reply. He seemed distracted, like a stranger to her. For the first time, she didn't know what to say to him.

The limousine left the freeway and eased into the city's shaded concrete canyons. Katie had a brief glimpse of one of Los Angeles's most famous hotels, and then, like a shy, nocturnal animal creeping into its burrow at sunrise, the gray car slipped into the stuffy darkness of an underground parking garage.

They wound around and around, going deeper and deeper beneath the hotel's steel-and-glass towers, until at last, on the lowest parking level, which was completely deserted, they rolled to a stop beside a pair of elevator doors marked "Private." Fergie got out and inserted a key into a lock in one of the doors. When they had slid silently open, Cole stepped out of the car and turned to offer Katie his hand. The look he gave her was enigmatic, full of irony.

The elevator was small, but plush. They rode together in silence, though Katie could feel Cole's eyes on her. He seemed tense, Katie thought, as if he were waiting for something to happen.

The elevator doors opened onto a small, carpeted foyer. It was softly lit by crystal wall sconces set on either side of a leaded glass mirror. In front of the mirror, on an exquisite antique table, sat a cut-crystal bowl filled with white roses.

Katie looked at Cole and raised her eyebrows. He

looked back at her and lifted a shoulder. "I can afford to hire people with taste," he said dryly.

The door to the foyer was opened by a square blond woman with Scandinavian cheekbones. As they moved past her she smiled warmly at them and murmured, "It's nice to have you back, Mr. Grayson."

Cole paused to give her shoulders a squeeze, then turned her toward Katie. "Nice to be back. Mrs. Jensen, I'd like you to meet Katherine—"

"K. T. Winslow! Oh, Miss Winslow," the housekeeper said, managing to sound both well-bred and thrilled to death, "it's such a pleasure to meet you. I recognized you from the *Tonight Show*. I've read all of your books."

Katie glanced at Cole and intercepted a grin. She knew he found it as funny as she did that his prim and proper housekeeper, obviously completely unimpressed by the fact that her employer was one of the biggest stars in the history of motion pictures, should have a bad case of hero worship concerning K. T. Winslow! His eyes were warm with amusement and delight.

Bemused, Katie smiled and murmured, "Why, thank you!" and moved on into the room.

Cole's apartment. The penthouse, obviously. It was huge, the view spectacular. And every square foot of the apartment was as beautifully and tastefully decorated as that tiny little jewel of a foyer. Cole might have hired the "people with taste" who were responsible for such perfection, but she had an idea that everything in this room, everything in the apartment, had had to meet his own personal standards.

She wandered to the window and stood looking out over the city, obscured now by the August haze. Behind her she could hear Cole and Mrs. Jensen quietly talking. After a moment she heard the door close, and turned to find Cole alone, watching her with a wry smile on his face. He made a little gesture with his hand and murmured, "Well, Katherine, welcome to my real life. How do you like it so far?"

Katie gazed at him and didn't answer.

"Actually," Cole drawled, strolling toward her, looking around as if he'd never seen the room before, "this is probably about as much like real life as what I do for a living. What percentage of the world's population do you suppose lives like this? Private limos, private elevators, glass towers."

She wanted to kick him. She wanted to jolt him out of this ridiculous "poor little rich boy" mood he seemed to be in. And yet somehow she knew it was more than that, that there was something else at the heart of it, something eating at *his* heart. And that she would have to be patient, and let him come to it in his own way, in his own time.

When she didn't answer, Cole glanced at his watch and said briskly, "Well, I've gotta go. Got a roomful of big shots waiting for me, and Fergie's keeping the motor running downstairs. Make yourself at home. You'd probably like to freshen up. Order whatever you'd like to eat—"

"Cole—"

"What?"

"What am I, your prisoner?" At the look on his face she said gently, "Cole, I don't live more than half an hour from here. Even if I'm going to stay here, I need a change of clothes—"

He snapped his fingers. "Damn! Knew I was forgettin' something. You *do* need clothes, don't you? Well, hell, there's all sorts of shops in this hotel—just call 'em and have 'em send up whatever you want."

"Cole," Katie said, laughing a little, "*I'm* not afraid to be seen in public. I even enjoy it. I consider shopping one of life's basic pleasures. I'll just—" Now it was her turn to snap her fingers. "Oh, damn."

"What's the matter?"

"I guess I am a prisoner, sort of. Seems I left most of my worldly goods, including my driver's license and credit cards, up on your mountaintop."

"No problem. Use mine." He took his wallet out of his hip pocket and tossed it onto the couch.

There was a little silence while Katie stared at it, and then she said evenly, "I'd rather not."

"Come on, Katherine." Cole's tone was dry, gently chiding. "False pride doesn't become you. We're friends, remember? Consider it a loan." He waited for her nod, then murmured, "Okay, then. Enjoy yourself. I'll be back around seven. We'll have dinner."

She nodded again, cleared her throat, and said, "Okay." Cole stood with his hand on the doorknob, just looking at her, almost, she thought, as if he were committing her to memory. A pulse began to throb in the pit of her stomach. She hated this, she thought.

He seemed so far away! Across the room . . . a million miles away. He was Cole, and yet he wasn't. He was a stranger who looked like Cole. He was someone she couldn't *touch*, couldn't imagine having kissed. Could it only have been last night that she'd stood naked in his arms? It seemed like another lifetime! She *hated* the strangeness!

Oh, but he looked so much like Cole, it made her ache to look at him. Hatless, with the pale strip of his forehead showing, but otherwise just as he'd been in the high country—cowboy boots, well-worn Levis, blue work shirt, hair a little too long . . . But in the high country he'd looked happy, relaxed, like a man in command of his life. Now there was a certain hardness about his jaw; tension lines were etched deep between his eyes and around his mouth. And his eyes . . . they still made Katie think of an eagle—fierce, golden, proud. But now there was sadness in them, too, and frustration . . . the eyes of an eagle in a cage.

Cole's mouth slipped into a smile, the one that didn't quite reach his eyes. "Buy something terrific," he said softly, and left her.

Buy something terrific. Katie stared after him, laughing, the hard, silent kind of laughter that hurt. What in the world would that mean to someone like Cole? To someone who'd go off to meet a "roomful of big shots" wearing a work shirt and Levis? And how like him that was, she thought on a wave of unanticipated tenderness that tightened her throat and made her eyes sting.

And how presumptuous to think she knew Cole Grayson well enough to believe something was "like" him! She'd known him a week. He'd told her she didn't know him at all. Right now there was a cold feeling in her stomach that told her he might be right.

Ten

At seven-fifteen, Cole was riding up in the elevator, sweating inside his tux and wondering whether he'd forgotten anything. He was late, but probably not enough to matter much. Dinner wouldn't be sent up until seven-thirty anyway. He hoped the flowers had arrived all right. He'd really had a time finding a florist who could produce poppies on such short notice.

Damn, he was nervous! He felt like a kid going to a prom. Except that, come to think of it, he'd never been to a prom.

In the foyer he paused to glance in the mirror, unnecessarily straightening his tie and smoothing down his hair. Then he took a deep breath, opened the door, and stepped inside.

Katherine was standing by the window, holding the flowers he'd sent. Poppies, scarlet, orange, and burgundy. She looked . . . radiant. She brought the sunshine into the room. The sight of her filled him with something that was both more and less than desire, something he recognized as *longing*.

She spoke first. "You got your hair cut. You look . . . wonderful." She sounded slightly out of breath.

"So do you." It occurred to him that he'd never seen her in a dress before. She was wearing black—something silky and clinging, with long sleeves and a deep V in front, a simple wrap style, caught at the waist with a starburst of rhinestones. It hugged her waist, subtly defined her breasts, and dropped in graceful folds over her hips to a point just below her knees. Her legs were long and slim, her heels pencil-thin and high enough to make her almost as tall as he was. The stark black set off her hair, and the poppies, to perfection. He'd never seen her hair like that, with most of the natural curl disciplined out of it, falling in rich crimson waves to her shoulders and beyond.

He cleared his throat, and said, "I like your hair like that. Matches the flowers."

Her smile lit up the whole room. Her laugh was a husky sound that rippled down his spine like silken fingers and turned his vague longings to good, old-fashioned lust. The temperature in the room went up several degrees.

"Uh . . ." he said, and was saved by the sound of the elevator doors. "Dinner," he announced, and went to admit a small, efficient army.

"That was fun," Katherine said, smiling at him as she held out her tiny porcelain cup. Cole filled it, and his, with warm sake and sipped in silence, watching the candle flames reflected in her eyes.

It was very quiet. The candles had burned halfway down. The waiters had gone, taking with them the chopsticks, the colorful array of small, harmonious dishes, the brazier and shabu shabu pot, and leaving them to their sake. The rice wine made a pool of warmth in his chest, but didn't touch the cold knot in the bottom of his stomach.

"Cole," Katherine said huskily, "you surprise me."

"Why?"

She gestured with her cup. "All this." She smiled. "I guess I had you pegged as a meat-and-potatoes man. Tell me something." Her smile faded; her gaze became direct and luminous. "Did you do this on purpose, to demonstrate how little I really know you?"

"Partly, I guess," Cole said. He held on to her eyes, while his hands toyed with the sake cup, turning it in aimless circles on the white tablecloth.

"So, you can eat with chopsticks." She lifted one shoulder, and her smile flicked briefly at the corners of her mouth. She sounded gently chiding when she added, "Cole, I do know that you spent time on location in both Japan and Southeast Asia."

"You've done your homework." He had to look away from her; she was too warm, too vivid. She made him ache with the need to hold her, to let her warm the cold places inside his heart. If he kept looking at her he'd change his mind. He'd let her go on believing he was some kind of hero. He'd pick her up in his arms and carry her to his bed and make love to her until he couldn't remember his own name, much less Mia's. Until he forgot the guilt, and the pain.

But he couldn't do that to her. She deserved more. She deserved *better*. So he filled up her cup with sake and said flatly, "What, exactly, do you know about Southeast Asia?"

She replied immediately. "It was your first major role—*Shanghai,* nineteen—"

"Statistics!" His laugh was harsh. "The stuff everybody knows. You can't make much of a book out of that, can you? Shall I give you something to write about, Ms. Winslow? Shall I give you the straight scoop on Cole Grayson? The *real* Cole Grayson? I promise you—a guaranteed best seller!" He glanced at her and saw that her eyes had gone wide and dark, and that her face was pale. He made a sound replete with self-disgust and pushed himself away from the table. Walked to the window. And from there, with his back to her, staring unseeingly across the diamond glitter of Los Angeles, he began to tell her about Mia.

He'd been very young. He told her that first, not as an excuse, but with a kind of wonder that it could have been so long ago. It still seemed like yesterday.

She was French and Indochinese, educated in Paris, but fluent in English. She'd come to work for the company as an interpreter. She seemed so poised, so elegant, with a natural grace and dignity that attracted him. *Class.* She had it, and it was what he wanted. But she had an unexpected capacity for fun, too, for play and for laughter. She made *him* laugh, which wasn't easy; he'd been taking himself pretty seriously, in those days.

She was beautiful, too, of course; taller than most Asians, with ivory skin and hair like black silk. It brushed her buttocks when she walked.

"So that's where—" Katherine said, and stopped abruptly, as if sorry for interrupting him.

Without turning around he nodded, and said simply, "Yes. I liked brushing it, braiding it. She did have . . . beautiful hair."

And he had loved her. He knew that now—probably he'd realized it even then, but still, he'd always been aware that when the time came, he'd leave her. The parting was bittersweet. He could still see her face, her eyes . . . the tears. But he'd been looking forward, and already she was becoming a part of his past. The movie was going to be a blockbuster, there was talk of Oscars, and his career was about to take off like a rocket. So he kissed her and promised to send for her, and went away and left her there.

For a while she wrote to him. And for a while he wrote back. But then the movie came out, the offers came in, and his life became very hectic. He was too busy to get into the hassle, the tangle of red tape required to bring Mia to the United States. He stopped writing. Her letters stopped coming. She became a sweet but waning memory.

And then, almost by chance, through mutual acquaintances, friends of friends, he found out that Mia had a child. His child. His daughter. He also learned that Mia wasn't well, that she'd had a difficult time of it after he'd left. He began the proceedings then, set the wheels in motion, but the wheels moved slowly. And before anything could come of it, he had word that Mia had died. No one seemed to know what had become of her child. His daughter. He hired private investigators to try to find her. Time went by, and it began to look hopeless, and then . . . his detectives reported that the child had been found in a Catholic orphanage. She was being cared for by nuns. She was safe and well. Cole was relieved. He was in the middle of filming a new movie and couldn't get away, but it seemed like she'd be all right where she was, until he could afford to take time off from his shooting schedule to go and see her.

"And then," he said bleakly, turning at last from the window, "the world—her world—went crazy." His eyes felt hot and dry; he rubbed them with his fingers, but it didn't help. "Her country was invaded, overrun. All ties with the West were cut, but word leaked out anyway. Words like . . . atrocities . . . genocide. Lord, Katherine. I've had people scouring the refugee camps ever since—nothing. *Nothing.*" He rubbed a hand over his face and turned back to the window. He felt tired . . . drained. "If, by some miracle, she's still alive, she'd be a grown woman by now. My daughter." He laughed, a harsh, ugly sound that hurt his throat. "The daughter I abandoned. The daughter I was too busy—"

"Cole—stop it!"

He looked at her, surprised by the anguish in her voice. She had her hand clamped over her mouth, and her eyes were bright with pain. "I'm sorry," he said softly. "I tried to tell you." He held out his hands. "Well, Katherine, here I am—complete with white hat. Some hero, huh?"

She took her hand away from her face, opened her

mouth, and closed it again, as if she just couldn't find anything to say. She did keep looking at him, though, and suddenly he knew he couldn't take the pain and accusation in those gray eyes another minute. He walked back to her slowly. Reached out his hand. Pulled it back before it could touch her hair.

"Katherine," he said, very, very gently, "I am sorry. I told you you were going to find out what sort of person I really am. Believe me, nobody's sorrier than I am. I might have been able to lie to my public all these years, but I couldn't lie to you." He looked at his watch, then leaned over and snuffed the candles with his fingers. "It's late, and I know this has been a long day—for both of us, I guess. Come on, I'll show you to your room. I had Mrs. Jensen fix one of the spares for you. In the morning, Fergie can take you wherever you need to go."

She rose without a word when he touched her elbow, and came unprotesting. She seemed dazed, which he could certainly understand. He knew this must have been a shock to her. No doubt she'd need some time to adjust her ideas about a few things. He just wished like hell he could have spared her this by being a different man with a different past.

It was a relief to put a door between himself and her eyes. After he'd pulled it shut he leaned on it and took several deep breaths. Then he went back to the living room and poured the last of the sake into his cup and drank it down in one gulp.

Katie was standing in the middle of the room to which she'd been so cavalierly dismissed, making up speeches. She did that when there was a lot she wanted to say to somebody, if she ever got the chance. She rarely delivered her speeches in person, but it made her feel better, somehow, to rehearse them.

There was so much she wanted to say to Cole, she didn't know where to begin! She was still stunned by what he'd told her, still in the grip of a devastating wave of empathy for him. Cole, she wanted to say, it was a tragedy, yes, a terrible tragedy. But there wasn't anything you could have done! You didn't know about the child! You tried to find her. You tried to get her out in time. You did all any man could have done, given the realities of bureaucracy. *Cole, it wasn't your fault!*

But in her heart she knew that all the speeches in the world wouldn't do any good. Cole had worn his guilt for so long, it had become part of him—like his costume, like the work shirt and Levis and cowboy boots. If he were ever to shed that guilt it wouldn't be because of any rationalizations she might have to offer. Like her fear of flying, his guilt wasn't rational.

What was it Cole had said to her? Something about having faith. And faith was believing. It was *feeling*, not thinking. She couldn't make it happen for him. If it was ever going to happen, he'd have to do it himself.

Katie found that intolerably frustrating.

For a while she went on standing there, at a loss to know what to do, knowing she had to do *something*. And then all at once she remembered something. Remembered words spoken on a summer night, in the middle of a river, under a canopy of stars . . .

She knew exactly what to do, but it wasn't easy. Her heart was pounding, her knees were weak and shaky, and her palms were cold and sweaty. It took every shred of will she had to kick off her shoes and march out of her room, down the hallway, and across the deserted living room to Cole's bedroom door.

She opened it without knocking. Cole had taken off his jacket. He stared at her, apparently frozen in the act of loosening his tie.

Katie closed the door and leaned against it. She swallowed a papery feeling in her throat and said, "Well," then stopped because her voice seemed to echo, as if she were shouting into a tunnel. She began again, speaking rapidly, trying to get it said before she lost her nerve completely. "You said if I still felt like making love with you after I knew all about you, I should let you know. So I'm letting you know. I do." She paused. Took a deep breath. "I just wanted to tell you. So I'll just . . . um." She turned and groped desperately for the doorknob.

The sound of its turning released Cole from freeze frame. He came to life, took one step toward her, and said hoarsely, "Katherine?"

"Of course," Katie said to the door panel, "I won't hold you to it if you've changed your mind. I just thought you ought to know—"

"Katherine, for goodness' sake, stop."

"I'm sorry. I'm talking because I don't know what else to do." She began to shiver, and held herself rigid, hoping he wouldn't notice.

His voice was very low, very soft. "What would you like to do?"

"I think . . ." She turned, lifted her head, and looked straight at him; took a deep breath in a vain attempt to stabilize her voice. "I think what I'd like to do is hold you."

His smile was gentle, rueful, poignant. It made her ache inside with the need to touch him. She wanted to put her hands on his face, smooth the fan of lines beside his eyes with her fingertips, touch the parentheses at the corners of his mouth with her lips. Why was it so hard to move forward? She felt as if the door, the wall, the whole building might fall down if she stopped propping them up.

Cole just said, "Katherine." He dropped his tie onto a chair and came toward her. Took her hands in his and held them for a moment, then lifted them to his mouth. His breath warmed them, then traveled in shivers down her arms, through her body, into her legs. His eyes were like searchlights, trying to see into her soul; trustingly, she opened it to him, letting him see all that was inside. After a moment, as if it were just too painful to look any more, he closed his eyes, placed her hands on his sides, and, with a deep sigh, gathered her close.

She pressed her hands to his back, absorbing the heat of his body through the smooth fabric of his shirt, feeling the rigidity in his muscles, the uncertain rhythms of his breathing. He held her gently, but with a quivering deep down inside, as if he were afraid of holding too tightly.

She lifted her face into the hollow of his neck, touching him with her lips, sliding her hands over his back, kneading, stroking. . . . His arms tightened around her, and one hand slipped upward to find the back of her neck under the heavy weight of her hair. His fingertips burrowed through her hair, subtly guiding her; in response, she brushed her lips across the hard ridge of his jaw, searching for his mouth.

They kissed as if they'd never done so before, lightly touching, savoring warmth and texture and shape, mingling breaths, teasing, exploring, becoming bolder, becoming hungrier, utterly lost in the wonder and awe of it.

Katie's chest hurt from the hammering her heart was inflicting on it. Something pushed upward into her throat, making it hurt there, too, making her lips tremble and her eyes sting.

Without pulling away from him she whispered, "It's been so long."

She could feel his smile with her lips. "Believe it or not, for me too."

"Really?"

"Really." He caressed her parted lips with his, a whole series of warm, sweet kisses that robbed her of breath, so that she finally had to pull away.

"Cole, I don't—I wish . . ."

"What, love?"

Her laughter was tremulous. "Oh, boy. What a sign of the times. I think I'm trying to apologize for chastity."

"That's okay." While one hand cradled her head, the other came to touch her face, lightly brush her cheek, then trail through her hair, tenderly combing it back away from her temple. His fingers burrowed deep into her hair and lay warm on her scalp, making of his hands a tender vise that held her firm under the weight of his scrutiny. "I think we're about to remedy that situation anyway. . . ."

She sighed, "Yes . . ." and waited, motionless, while his head slowly descended.

His mouth covered hers, his tongue opened her, entered her. She felt the penetration deep inside, a hot shaft that went straight to the center of her body and exploded in star bursts through all her nerves. She gasped, and his tongue drove deeper. She forgot about the need to breathe, forgot she had arms and legs. All she knew was his mouth, and the fiery ache inside her. . . .

When he left her mouth it felt cold, bereft. She felt his lips on her forehead and leaned against them, shaking. "Oh," she said, a small, helpless sound somewhere between a laugh and a whimper. "What now?"

His body was shaking, too, partly with laughter. "Don't you know?"

"Oh Cole, I feel so dumb. So scared. I feel like I've never done this before."

"You haven't." He stroked her hair, her throat, drew his thumb across her moisture-glazed lips. He was smiling, but his eyes were molten gold. "Neither have I. This is a first for both of us. The first time you loved me . . ." His voice grew ragged, and the words sighed against her mouth. "The first time I loved you . . ."

Eleven

. . . The first time I loved you.

She knew he hadn't meant it like that, but it sang in her heart anyway: *I love you. I love you, Cole; I love you.* It filled up her heart the way he filled her arms, her mouth, until there was no other reality. *I love you, Cole.*

The world stopped spinning; the universe came down to the small circle their arms made, holding each other. The center of that universe was his mouth and hers. It expanded to encompass his hands as they found the zipper on her dress and slowly drew it down . . . as they kneaded the rounds of her shoulders and followed the gentle curve of her spine to where it dipped inward, then out again.

His chin nudged hers. He whispered something she couldn't understand, and found the hollow under her jaw with his mouth. She turned her head, baring the vulnerable arch of her throat, gasping when his mouth moved over it, hot and open, measuring her pulse with his tongue. His lips trailed across her collarbone, his breath sending shivers into her breasts, making her nipples hard and sensitive, making her yearn for the pressure of his hands.

She stirred restlessly, tugging at her dress, wanting firmer, rougher textures against her skin. He made another of those soft, wordless sounds and touched her bared shoulder delicately with his mouth, asking her in the most loving of ways to be patient. Then *he* undressed her, making an erotic adventure of it, discovering her body inch by inch, mapping her with his hands, his lips, his tongue.

Sensation filled her up and overflowed; her breathing was shallow, because there was no room inside her for breath. She swallowed, licked her lips, muttered, "Cole . . . I don't think I can stand up anymore." The words were slurred; it was hard to move her lips. All her bones and muscles seemed to have melted. She gave a grateful little chuckle when he lifted her into his arms.

Cole chuckled too. "Well, now," he said huskily, "I think we've been here before."

He was remembering the way he'd carried her in his arms, just a few short days ago; remembering how good she'd felt then, and how amused he'd been by his surprising physical response to her. He hadn't known then that she was going to become special to him in ways that had very little to do with anything physical. And he'd forgotten what kind of effect that "specialness" could have on physical responses, deepening them . . . compounding, expanding, augmenting . . . until he felt awed by the intensity of his own emotions. He almost wished he could backtrack a few notches to something less complicated, like simple, straightforward *passion*. He hadn't bargained for this. And it scared him, more than a little bit.

"Katherine," he said, looking down at her, braving the depths of her eyes, "from this point on it's uncharted territory for us."

"Well, that's true," she whispered, "but I think it's too late to turn back."

His chuckle became a groan. "That's for sure!"

"It's all right. It's not the first time you've taken me with you into the unknown."

"No?"

"No." Her smile began in a small way. "Twice you took me riding on the wind, remember? The first time I saw a sunrise, and the second time I touched a cloud." Her voice caught, and became uneven. "I can't wait—"

He didn't let her finish. Something that had been building inside him since the moment she'd walked into his room finally burst the bonds of the little self-control he had left. He lifted her hard into his kiss, smothering the rest of her sentence with his mouth, trapping both words and breath in her throat. She gave a fierce little growl and met the hungry thrusts of his tongue with her own, and Cole knew quite suddenly that it was time to find a more comfortable place for them both.

When he laid her on his bed she stirred languorously, sinuously, watching him with lips parted and eyes glazed with passion. Whatever shyness she'd had, whatever fears and reservations, they were gone now. She was wanton as a kitten, trusting him enough to let him know how much she wanted him.

He moved away from her to undress, but she reached for him, whispering raggedly, "Please . . . let me." But her fingers weren't adept enough, or fast enough for him, and she had to be content with helping, with running her hands over each newly bared part of his body, covering it with kisses. She couldn't seem to get enough of touching him, kissing him, and that filled him with a kind of wonder. He'd never known anyone like her before—a woman more anxious to give than to receive. In his experience, women tended to be passive, to expect him to perform miracles. It stunned him to hear her say, "Please, Cole, I want to touch you with my mouth."

But very soon the lines between giving and receiving blurred and became unimportant. He was on fire, aching with the need to be inside her. It was time to take control. So he turned her onto her belly and rolled her under him, covering her with the full length of his body, reaching under her to caress her breasts, her belly, her thighs, until she could only gasp and gasp. When he turned her again she was trembling and helpless, sobbing his name in complete surrender.

Except that, in entering her, he felt that it was *he* who surrendered. There was no more giving, no more taking, just sharing. He knew a moment of peace, of complete calm, as if he'd come into the eye of a storm.

Katherine was quiet too; even her breath seemed suspended as her body relaxed and adjusted to the newness of him. Her eyes were closed, her lashes lying dark on moisture-dewed skin. Her lips parted in a smile as she whispered, "Oh . . ." He felt her hands on his face, touching him tenderly, lovingly.

Wordlessly he lowered his mouth to her throat. He felt her sigh and arch upward, adjusting her body to his, seeking an even greater closeness. He caught her to him and felt her legs come around him, felt her pulse quicken and her breathing become ragged.

The eye of the storm had passed. With renewed intensity it caught them up and carried them beyond reason, into a realm of pure sensation. It left them battered, exhausted, sated . . . and more than a little awed.

Sometime during the quiet that followed the storm, Katherine licked her swollen lips and mumbled, "Hmm . . . Now, that's what I'd call riding a tempest."

Cole said, "What?" and laughed a little as he kissed her. She laughed, too, and murmured, "Never mind. It's just the romance writer in me, I guess. Sorry."

But Cole was thinking that, from this day forward, there was going to be a certain romance writer inside him too.

• • •

It's never really dark in the city. Katie thought how odd it was that city lights, which number only a few million—an infinitesimal number, compared to the stars—can still turn the night to a milky gray that masks color and makes everything look flat, like an old black-and-white movie.

She'd slept for a little while in Cole's arms—a catnap induced by a kind of feline lethargy and terminated abruptly by one of those disconcerting involuntary jerks. Now she lay awake, making these and other discoveries about the night, too full of miracles to sleep. Too full of the miracle of Cole . . .

Cole. He was there, his body warm against her back, and yet she knew this couldn't be real. Nothing could be so wonderful. No one could be this happy. It was terrifying, to be so happy, because she knew it couldn't possibly last forever, and she didn't want it ever to end.

A sob shuddered silently through her. Cole's hand moved on her rib cage, lightly stroking. His soft question stirred the hair near her ear. "Katherine . . . what's the matter?"

"Oh—Cole. Are you awake?"

"No. I talk in my sleep."

"Did I wake you?"

"No. I've been lying here, listening to your breathing."

"How fascinating."

"Yeah. Katherine . . . are you crying?"

"No."

He raised himself on one elbow and touched his lips to her eyelid. "Then why are your eyelashes wet?" His hand moved slowly down her arm from her shoulder to her elbow and back again, the lightest of caresses.

"I'm not crying. I'm just happy. And . . ." She turned blindly into his arms, burying her face in the soft hair on his chest. "Oh, Cole . . . I'm scared."

His arms tightened convulsively around her. "Again? I thought we'd gotten past that."

"It's just . . . it's terrifying to feel like this."

He didn't answer, but held her so tightly, she could hardly breathe, and pressed his cheek against the top of her head. After a moment he lay back with a sigh, pulling her with him, settling her comfortably on his chest.

But she couldn't stay still. Turning in the circle of his arm, she raised herself on one elbow to look down at him, studying his face in the gray light. "Cole, tell me the truth." She touched his face wonderingly, mapping his features with her fingertips, one by one. "Are you real?"

His laughter bumped his chest against her breasts as he rolled her over to cover his body full length. "Oh, yeah, I'm real. Either that, or you've got some imagination, woman!"

She began to laugh, too, and moved her body upon his in an allover caress. His hands slid down her back, following the curve of her spine all the way to its beginnings. "Cole," she murmured huskily, "I adore you."

"*Hush.*" The muscles in his torso contracted under her as he lifted his head to stop her words with a kiss. "Adoration is for heroes." His hands tightened briefly on her bottom, then slipped down to the backs of her thighs. "I'm not a hero—just a man."

"So I noticed," Katie said, swallowing a small gasp. At the behest of his hands she moved her legs to lie along the outsides of his. "However . . ." She lowered her head to touch his lips with the lightest of kisses. "Heroism is in the eye of the beholder. Like beauty— which, by the way, I also happen to think you have."

"You do, do you?" His laughter rocked her gently. Still holding her thighs in his firm grasp he raised himself to tease her mouth and throat with kisses. "Crazy woman."

Yes, she was. That contact was driving her crazy, making it harder and harder to breathe. "If you think that's bad"—she gasped, arching her head back as his mouth found the vulnerable curve of her throat—"I'm also . . . crazy in lo—"

"No." It was a growl, a groan, raw with passion and pain. With that one word and the pressure of his mouth he silenced her, trapping her words inside her.

Frustrated, she felt the words resound inside her and erupt in a fiery explosion of physical desire. *I love you, Cole.* Since she couldn't tell him with words, there was nothing left for her to do but show him.

Katie woke at last to early-morning daylight, hazy and soft, an unfamiliar time of day for her. Beside her Cole still slept, on his back, but turned slightly toward her, and for a long time she lay still, studying his face.

A true test of a woman's feelings for a man, she reflected in tender amusement, must be the ability to look upon him softly snoring, jaws bristling with stubble, and still feel her heart turn cartwheels.

My heart will still be turning cartwheels, Katie thought, when we are both old and his teeth are resting independently in a jar.

Needing to reassure herself by touching him, she reached toward the lock of hair that had fallen across his forehead, then slowly drew her hand back without waking him. It was one thing for her to see *his* unguarded face first thing in the morning, but *her* face, in its natural, forty-year-old condition, wasn't something she cared to present to anyone. Cole could talk all he wanted to about the unimportance of appearances, but there were a few illusions she preferred to try to maintain as long as possible!

She eased herself carefully out of bed and walked naked to the window, hoping to find the sunrise. It was there, on the other side of the hotel, but mirrored in the windows and glass facades of skyscrapers. She stood and watched the buildings turn from softest pink to warm butterscotch, to fiery brilliance that hurt her eyes, making them sting and water.

Oh, God, she thought, crossing her arms over the

cold knot of fear in her belly. What was to become of her if he wouldn't let her love him?

It would be all right, she told herself, taking new heart, like a poppy, from the rising sun. He just didn't believe she really meant it. He must have heard those words so many times before. She'd just have to make him believe it. She'd just have to tell him again, and this time make him listen.

With both spirit and resolve restored, she went off to her own room to shower and dress, humming "You Are My Sunshine" under her breath.

When the door had closed behind her, Cole sat up and reached for the telephone. As he ordered breakfast he was thinking about the night, and about waking to the sight of Katherine in nude silhouette against a dawn sky, hair tumbling down her back, lifting her arms like a pagan goddess to greet the morning. And as always, he knew it wasn't so much the sight of her that affected him so, as it was the way he felt, watching her. She lifted his spirits, filled him with warmth and joy and tenderness.

He dropped the telephone receiver back into its cradle and covered his face with his hands, rubbing his eyes and the stubble on his jaw. She made him feel happy, and ridiculously young. And what in the world was he going to do about her?

He knew she thought she was in love with him, and he just couldn't let it happen. He'd been inexcusably irresponsible to let it go this far. He still wasn't quite sure how he felt about her, but he did know she deserved better than he could give her—a casual affair, at best. The demands of his career and the pressures of being who he was would get in the way of anything deeper and ultimately destroy it, and possibly even destroy her. As it had destroyed Mia. As he'd seen it destroy so many other relationships. Oh, he knew there were successful long-term relationships in Hollywood, but they were the exceptions; it took a very special kind of person, and a very deep commitment, to make it work. He'd already proven, at terrible cost, that he didn't have what it took, and trying it again just wasn't worth the risk. It sure wasn't worth risking Katherine for.

So no matter what it cost him, no matter how much it hurt her, he knew he had to put her out of his life. Under the circumstances that wasn't going to be easy, but for once the demands of his career were going to work to his advantage. This new project—his first as director—was going to require all his concentration and energy, and the trip to Africa had come at the right time. . . .

Feeling resolved, and indescribably bleak, Cole got up and went into the bathroom to shower and shave.

When he came out again, breakfast had arrived. Katherine was standing beside the small, linen-draped table, holding a long-stemmed red rose, touching its petals to her cheek. She was wearing tan slacks and a yellow blouse, and had her hair swept back into a neat coil on the nape of her neck. She looked sleek and elegant, but Cole found subtle reminders of last night's wanton in her flushed cheeks, her slightly parted lips, and in the husky rasp of her voice that even now could stir the banked fires in his loins.

"Good morning," she said, turning.

Warming himself with her smile, he answered, " 'Mornin', sunshine."

The smile grew radiant. "Do you have any idea what a lovely greeting that is? It makes me *feel* like sunshine."

Unable to stop himself, he went to her and put his arms around her, catching the rose between their bodies. He glanced down at it, then back at her face, and said brusquely, "I guess they couldn't manage poppies this morning."

"It's okay . . . it's beautiful. Thank you." The rose lay between his lips and hers; with a sigh he nudged it down, out of the way, then kissed her softly, delicately, as if her mouth were as fragile as its petals. She held her breath, as if beholding a miracle.

Aching inside, Cole whispered, "How are you?"

She whispered back, "Fine." There was a breathy catch in her voice. Turning out of his arms, she reached to put the rose back in its silver bud vase, then poured orange juice from a crystal decanter into a crystal goblet and handed it to him. She poured another for herself and lifted it, smiling, to touch his.

"Katherine," he murmured, toasting her. With equal solemnity she responded, "Cole."

They both drank, and, after a long moment of silent communion, sat down to breakfast. Katherine seemed pensive when she poured coffee from a silver pot, as if there were something she was trying to figure out how to say. Cole thought he knew what she wanted to say. He was trying to think of a way to keep her from doing it, when she surprised him.

Her eyes crinkled thoughtfully at him over her coffee cup. "Cole, why do you always call me Katherine?"

Caught off-guard, he answered more abruptly than he meant to. "It's your name, isn't it?"

"Yes, but I have several others—Kate, Katie—even, heaven forbid, *Kathy.* Except for my mother, whenever she was annoyed with me, you're the only person I've ever known who calls me Katherine."

Since it seemed that she really wanted to know, he gave the question a moment's consideration, then shrugged and said simply, "It suits you." She looked away, clearly unsatisfied, so he hesitated a moment longer and then went on. "Katie is a little girl, and Kate is"—he searched briefly for a word, and settled for—"*plain.* But Katherine is a name for a woman. A beautiful, mature woman. It's a queen's name—it has class, style, elegance." And then, because under the circumstances he felt uncomfortable talking like that, he shrugged and concluded flatly, "It suits you."

She stared at him for so long, he wondered if she'd somehow misunderstood. Then she carefully put her cup back onto its saucer and said in a shaken whisper, "Is that . . . really how you see me?"

Dear Lord, he thought, doesn't she *know*? "Yes, of course—don't you?" When she just looked at him he said more gently, "I thought you told me you'd made yourself into what you are. Didn't you know what you were making?"

She gave a funny little laugh and got up from the table. "Well, I knew what I wanted to be, but I never really thought I'd made it—I guess because I never really felt it . . . in *here*." She turned to face him, her hand curled into a fist and pressed against her stomach. "Inside I always felt the same, like dumpy little Katie."

Very softly Cole said, "And now?"

"Right now, for the first time, I really feel like *Katherine*." She went on looking and looking at him. Cole felt as if he were up to his neck in quicksand. "Cole," she said very slowly, "I have to tell you something."

In a strangled voice he said, "Katherine—" but she put out her hand in a gesture that was almost supplication.

"No, please, Cole. I know you'd rather I didn't, but I have to. It's so terrible to have to keep it inside. I have an idea this is not going to come as a surprise to you, but I love you. I also have an idea you've heard that before, but I have to tell you that what I feel for you isn't just hero worship or some sort of stupid crush." Her laugh was low, and held a kind of awe. "My feelings for you have layers, colors, textures, dimensions you wouldn't even believe." She lifted her shoulders and finished softly, "I know it wasn't a very smart thing to do, but I've done it anyway. I've fallen in love with you."

Harshly, almost angrily, feeling as if the words had thorns, Cole said, "I wish you hadn't done that."

Very gently, almost in sympathy, she said, "I know. But Cole, I don't expect you to love me back." She paused, took a careful breath. "All I need, all I want, is for you to let me love you."

All that he was feeling erupted in a sharp cry of rejection. He turned away from her. "For God's sake, Katherine . . . don't."

"Why not?"

He turned back, so full of fury, he wanted to shake her; so full of pain, he wanted to put his arms around her and hold on to her and never let her go. . . . "Look at you!" His voice was raw; it hurt his throat. "Look at what you are, all you have to give! For God's sake, don't waste yourself, don't diminish yourself! Go find someone who deserves you, someone who can give you something back besides heartaches! Don't waste it on me."

Very quietly she said, "Don't you think I should be the one to decide who I give myself to? It's taken me longer than some to get here, but I am a grown woman. I make my own choices, Cole."

She was standing very straight, with her head high and proud. She made him feel small and fraudulent. "Katherine," he whispered, "I can't give you what you want. I'm sorry."

"How do you know what I want?"

"I know what you *deserve*, and it sure isn't me, or the kind of life you'd have with me! Look at this—this is no kind of life at all. I live in a cage, Katherine—a cage of my own making, true, but a cage all the same. I can't go to a restaurant, I can't go walking down a city street, I can't see a play or go dancing or walk into a drugstore to buy a newspaper! This life destroys relationships, Katherine—it chews them up and spits them out. It destroys *people*. I thought—I tried to make that clear to you last night."

"And I thought I made myself clear last night, too, Cole. I choose who I will love. I think the other choices—the ones that go with that—are mine to make as well."

"No." He took a deep breath. "They aren't." He looked straight at her, though it hurt more than he'd have thought possible. "Katherine, I'm leaving for Africa. Tonight. I'm going to be there for a while—four or five months, longer if the weather doesn't cooperate. It's a new project, my first as director. It's going to keep me very, very busy." *Busy enough, please, God, to let me forget her . . .*

"I see," she said, so quietly, he knew that she understood. She stood very still, just looking at him, and after a moment he saw something move on her cheek. One solitary tear, trickling slowly down.

"Katherine," he said raggedly. "For God's sake, don't."

She shook her head and brushed at her cheek, then stared at her fingers as if surprised by the moisture on them. "Oh, Cole," she said, and gave a sad little laugh. "Don't you know this isn't for me? It's you I'm crying for. You know, there was a time when I'd have thought it was me. I'd have thought it was some lack in me— that I wasn't classy enough, or pretty enough, or good enough in bed."

"Katherine—"

"But now I know there's nothing the matter with me. I know I'm the best thing that ever happened to you, Cole Grayson. And what's more, you know it too. And you're blowing it. So I'm crying for you, because you're throwing away something wonderful."

Barely whispering, Cole said, "Katherine, don't you understand? I just can't let you—"

"Oh, yes," she said gently. "I do understand. You can't let me love you. You can't let anyone love you— not the people who work with you and for you, not your fans, the public—not anyone. Because you think you don't deserve to be loved. It's funny—you keep telling me you aren't a hero, that you're only a man, but you don't believe it. You failed once, didn't live up to your idea of what Cole Grayson was supposed to be—superman. Look, I've got news for you: Making mistakes is what makes you a man. And here's something else, while I'm passing out so many profound words of wisdom: Making mistakes doesn't disqualify you from deserving love. In fact, I'd say that the more people screw up, the more love they need!"

She turned abruptly, brushing angrily at her cheeks

with both hands. He heard her whisper, "Dammit. I promised myself I wouldn't do this."

There was a long silence, while Cole stared down at his coffee cup and his heart sat in his chest like a stone and his arms ached with emptiness. After a while Katherine took a deep breath and said, "Cole, I think it's best if I go now. I still don't have my driver's license or credit cards, or any money, for that matter, so I'd appreciate it if you could have someone drive me—"

"I'll call Fergie."

"Thank you."

"I'll see that you get your things."

"I know you will. I think I'll wait downstairs in the lobby, so could you ask Fergie to pick me up out front?" She laughed a little, but shakily; it ended with a sniff. "I may be crazy, but I think it's *fun* to be picked up by a limo."

It was hard to believe she was leaving. She'd been a part of his life for a little more than a week, but he felt her going as if he were being pulled up by the roots. He sat very still and rigid, holding himself together.

At the door she paused. "Cole, I'm sorry. There's just one thing I have to know. Last night . . . why did you let it happen?"

A knife plunged into his belly and twisted. Before he could stop himself he'd blurted out, "Dammit, Katherine, that was before I knew how much I—"

"I think I understand." Her eyes were luminous with sadness. "That was before you knew how much you loved me."

Twelve

Katie did everything she'd told herself she'd do.

As soon as her wallet arrived she took herself on a monumental shopping spree, during which she not only completely restructured her wardrobe, but also traded in her prosperous-looking but sedate Buick for a two-seater Mercedes. It was eight years old, but it was a Mercedes, and a sports car to boot. Her insurance agent and her accountant both had fits.

She called her children and had nice long-distance visits with both of them. They talked about school, of course, and the weather in the East. They talked about grades (theirs) and books (hers) and love affairs (theirs!). She told them about her new car. They asked about Cole Grayson. They wanted to know how it felt to meet the biggest movie star in the world. "Fine," Katie said. "Just great. He turned out to be a very interesting man."

Kelly's response was, "Interesting? Mom, is that all you have to say about meeting one of the world's most eligible, not to mention gorgeous—"

"Darling, isn't he a little out of your age bracket?"

To which her daughter had replied, "Mother, Cole Grayson is a man for *all* ages!"

Christopher had let a small silence pass and then asked quietly, "Mom? Is everything okay?"

"Yes," she'd told him, swallowing twice. "Of course. It's going to be a terrific book."

"Mom. Do you want to talk about it?"

"No, darling, not now. Maybe someday."

"Okay," her son had said. "Mom? Love you . . ."

When she had recovered from that, she called her agent, Sonya. They went to lunch and talked about editors and contracts and royalty checks and the reviews of Katie's latest book.

Katie had a glass of wine with lunch, which wasn't unusual, and then a second, which was. Over the third, she began to tell Sonya about Cole.

"I know what you're thinking," she said sometime later, peering moodily into her wineglass.

Warm and wise, Sonya smiled, and said kindly, "You do, do you?"

"Yeah. I'm a real dummy, developing a crush on a movie star. Really stupid. Only . . . dammit—" She brought her hand down smartly on the tabletop and was mildly startled but not much concerned when Sonya calmly reached over to rescue her silverware. "I haven't even thought of him like that in . . . ages. Sonya, this is not a crush. I swear to God it's not. I really *love* him. I love him so many different ways, it isn't even *funny*. I love him—"

"Katie," Sonya said, patting her hand. "I believe you. But Elizabeth Barrett Browning has already said it much better."

Katie put a hand over her eyes and groaned. "Do you know how awful it is to love somebody so much, and have him not let you? Lord, it's so *frustrating*. Sonya, what am I going to do?"

"Well," her agent said mildly, putting on her glasses and peering over them at the check, "I'll tell you what

I've told you before when you've been in rough waters emotionally—what I tell all my writers." She looked up at Katie and smiled, and Katie laughed painfully and joined her voice to Sonya's in rueful chorus: " 'Put it in a book'! I know, I know. Oh, Sonya," she mumbled, sniffling into her napkin, "what would I do without you?"

"I don't know," Sonya murmured, taking a firm grip on Katie's elbow as she got up from the table, deftly preventing catastrophe involving a water glass.

"There are times," she said dryly, giving Katie's waist a squeeze as she handed her carefully into a cab, "when I don't know whether I'm a literary agent or a house mother for a sorority. Put it all into the book, Katie. Channel your emotions into creative energy. This book is going to be dynamite."

The trouble was, Katie was caught in a dilemma. She was pretty sure she wasn't going to die from this, though she was quite sure she would never get over *loving* Cole. But she knew she could eventually put it behind her and get on with her life and manage to be a whole and happy person again—if she could just get him out of her mind, her heart, her life! But how could she get Cole Grayson out of her mind and her heart when he was still so much a part of her life? Day in and day out, for the next four months, waking and sleeping, she was going to have to live and breathe . . . Cole Grayson!

Before leaving for Africa (running away, Katie called it), Cole had arranged for her to have free run of both his worlds. At the studios, she found that she wasn't only given access to practically everyone who had ever known or worked with Cole, but that she was wholeheartedly welcomed. She interviewed literally hundreds of people—from producers, directors, mega-stars, and studio moguls, to cameramen, technicians, makeup artists, and wardrobe mistresses, all the way down to the lowliest script girl. Nearly everyone seemed to be just dying to have a chance to talk about Cole. A straw poll probably would have revealed that many believed Cole Grayson could walk on water.

Graciously declining the use of both the limo and Cole's various aircraft, Katie drove herself to Cole's ranch, where she spent a wonderful and poignant two weeks renewing her acquaintance with Birdie and Snake, Sunday and Chipmunk and Frankie, and all the rest of the cowboys, now back from the high country. It was especially good to see Billy Claude, home from the hospital and already playing his guitar again and working with Diablo as if the accident had never happened.

She had a chance to get better acquainted with Cole's older brother, Rob, the quiet-spoken man she'd met briefly that night at the river, when he'd driven the truck out to pick them up and wound up having to change two flat tires. She met his wife, Jenna, too, and found her to be as friendly and outspoken as her husband was reserved. She discovered that Cole had two nephews. One was a commercial airline pilot. The other was in New York, studying acting and trying to make it on Broadway without letting anyone know about his family "connection." Katie and Jenna traded their sons' addresses and telephone numbers, to pass along.

By the time she was ready to go back to Malibu and get to work writing the book, she was pretty sure she knew Cole as well as anybody in the world. And she'd discovered that the better she knew him, the more she found in him to respect and admire. In short, the better she understood him, the more she loved him.

Forget Cole? Impossible. To her he was more *human* now than ever, and seemed even more real. Her mental image of him was sharper and more vivid now than the day he'd left for Africa. Perhaps, Katie thought, because her memory wasn't obscured by tears . . .

Her sensory memories hadn't dimmed with time and his absence, either. How much longer, she wondered, would she lie awke at night, with the taste of him on her lips, feeling the soft-firm pressure of his mouth on her body, the resilience of his muscles beneath her hands . . . while her belly knotted and twisted, her blood raced, and her pulse throbbed with frustrated desire? How long would she see his smile, hear his voice, feel his arms holding her? How long was she going to wake up in the middle of the night to lie staring into the darkness, shaking with loneliness and . . . yes, dammit, *anger*?

She finished the book the week before Christmas. She made four copies of the manuscript. Two went straight to her publisher by air express; another she mailed fourth class to Sonya; the last she bound in manuscript covers, wrapped carefully in brown paper, and had delivered by messenger to Cole's ranch. That done, she packed a suitcase and drove herself to the airport, where she caught a flight to New York, to spend Christmas with her children.

Two days before Christmas there was a storm in the Northeast that tied the entire eastern seaboard in knots. A foot of snow fell on New York City. Airline flights were canceled; commuter traffic ground to a halt. On Christmas Eve, New York lay silent under a blanket of white.

On Christmas Day, right after breakfast, Katie, Kelly, and Christopher left their hotel and walked to the park. They made angels in the snow, and a snowman, and lost an all-out, no-holds-barred snowball war to three little boys and an enormous, exuberant dog.

Walking home on numbed, clumpy feet, with cheeks raw and red, eyes sparkling, and noses running, words puffing vapor clouds into the cold air, they talked about what a great Christmas it was—one of the very best ever.

"It's the snow," Kelly declared, throwing her head back and her arms out and turning a clumsy pirouette. "Snow just *makes* Christmas."

"Oh, I don't know," Chris said thoughtfully. "I think it's just being together like this. All of us."

There was a little silence while they all thought of

David, spending Christmas in Virginia with his new wife and her family. Then out of the blue Chris said, "Mom, do you think you'll ever get married again?"

Katie laughed, ducked her head to blow on her hands. "Oh, heavens—I don't know!"

Kelly, always emphatically opinionated, declared, "Well, I think you ought to."

Katie said mildly, "If I find someone I feel like marrying, I'm sure you'll be one of the first to know."

Chris looked sideways at her, but didn't say anything.

They plodded along the slushy sidewalk, blowing feathery puffs of vapor. After a while Kelly tilted her head thoughtfully to one side and said, "I think you should at least buy a real house, Mom. Keep the condo—it's great to have a place at the beach—but don't you think it would be nice to have a house—someplace where it snows in the wintertime, in the mountains maybe. A place with trees, even a few horses?"

Katie managed a helpless laugh, and murmured, "Oh, Kelly . . ."

Christopher put his arm around her and gave her shoulders a squeeze.

Cole tiptoed through the kitchen like a cat burglar, put his hands over Birdie's eyes, and whispered, "Merry Christmas."

As he'd known she would, she shrieked blue murder and darn near decked him.

"Cole! What are you doin', comin' home Christmas Eve without tellin' a soul! You're supposed to be in Africa! You damn near scared me to death! What are you doin' down here in the cookhouse instead of up at the big house with the folks?"

"Nobody's home at Rob and Jenna's. Still at church, I guess. And my place is—"

"All closed up and cold—and whose fault is that? You coulda called, you . . . you—"

"Aw, come on, Birdie, wish me a Merry Christmas. I brought you a present."

"No!"

"Sure, I did."

"Where is it? Something from Africa?"

"You'll have to wait till tomorrow morning, just like everybody else. Speaking of which, where *is* everybody? It's Christmas Eve!"

"Well, now, Cole, it's almost midnight, too. Where do you suppose people are? Rob and Jenna, they went to the midnight service at the church, like they always do, and everybody else who has good sense has gone to bed." Birdie suddenly tittered, shaking all over. "Waitin' for Santa Claus!"

Cole laughed, too, remembering so many other long-ago Christmastimes and "waiting for Santa Claus."

Lord, it was good to be home. Outside the air was cold and frosty, the sky sparkling with stars. There was no snow this year, but it felt like winter, at least, and in here in Birdie's kitchen it was warm and smelled of mincemeat and pumpkin and sage.

"What are *you* doing still up, then?" he asked Birdie, though he knew the answer. There were pies in the oven; he could smell them. Birdie remembered the pies, too, just in the nick of time, and went to take them out of the oven.

"So," Cole asked, coming up behind her to steal a taste of corn-bread stuffing from the dishpan on the counter. "Who's around this Christmas?"

Birdie slapped at Cole's hand—it was part of the ritual—and considered. "Chipmunk went to his sister's, and Sunday and Clara have kinfolks comin' for dinner. Most everybody else is here—all my family, and, of course, Billy Claude."

"How is he?"

"Mended fine. Sunday says he's got that black horse of yours jumping through a hoop."

"No kiddin'. I brought him a present, too—got him an African guitar. Only has one string."

Birdie shook with laughter. "Well, if there's music in it, that boy'll find it!"

"Yeah."

"Yeah, that Billy Claude . . ." They were silent, reviewing memories. Cole's were full of a red head and a blond one leaning close, gleaming in the firelight, and two voices harmonizing old songs.

Birdie got very busy, arranging pies on cooling racks. Cole fiddled, picking up a potholder to examine the scorch marks on it as if they were of gravest importance. He wasn't going to ask if *she'd* been here—he knew she would have been—and Birdie wasn't going to mention her unless he did.

"Oh, by the way, Cole," Birdie said casually. "Somebody sent you a present."

"Oh?"

"Yeah . . . came a few days ago. Messenger brought it." She put down the potholders, wiped her hands on a dish towel, and moved to the rolltop desk, taking her sweet time about it. Shoving back the desk top, she picked up a bulky brown package, hefted it once, and plunked it into Cole's hands. "Here it is."

He held it, looking down at his own name and address printed in block letters in marking pen. He didn't recognize the printing, but he'd read enough scripts to know a manuscript when he had one in his hands. It gave him a funny feeling, almost a numbness, as if he'd become suspended in time and space.

"Well?" Birdie said. "Ain't you gonna open it?"

"What? Oh . . . yeah. I'll open it. Later." He tucked the package under his arm and leaned over to give Birdie a kiss. "Better be goin' to bed myself, I guess, or else Santa Claus never will come. Merry Christmas, Birdie."

"Cole?" He stopped, but didn't turn around. He knew he wouldn't be able to lie to those shrewd black eyes. "You never did say—what made you decide to come home?"

"Africa was too hot," he said flatly. "Just didn't feel

like Christmas." He waited, but Birdie didn't say anything, so he went out, shutting the door softly behind him.

Outside, the moon was up and the air crackled with frost. His footsteps crunched loudly on the gravel road. He let himself into his dark, empty house, but instead of going to bed, built a fire in the big stone fireplace in the study. When it was really roaring, he sat down on the floor in front of it and began to take the brown paper wrapping off of his Christmas present.

It was New Year's Day, the kind of southern California January day that makes people in places like Chicago and Buffalo and Milwaukee turn off their television sets in the middle of the Rose Bowl game and start calling travel agents and real-estate brokers.

Katie and Loretta, her secretary, were trying to get a head start on the year by catching up on everything that had gotten shoved aside during the rush to finish *Hero.* Loretta, whose husband was an ex-linebacker for UCLA, was always delighted with an excuse to get out of the house on New Year's Day. She'd brought along an extra container of taco dip and a bag of tortilla chips. During the course of the morning, both it and the piles of Christmas cards and fan letters slowly diminished.

A little after noon, Loretta stretched and tipped her chair back on two legs—a habit Katie had been trying in vain to break her of. She turned her head, yawning, to gaze out the window, and the chair came back to its original position with a loud thump.

"Who in the world," she exclaimed, "is *that?*"

Katie was frowning over a semiliterate fan letter. "Who is what?"

"Come here," Loretta said. "You won't believe this. Some guy is coming up the street on a *horse.*"

Katie sat very still. Loretta was standing at the casement window, looking down on the winding brick streets, walkways, and flower beds of the townhouse complex.

"Who *is* that? He looks like something out of a western movie!"

Katie stood up slowly and walked to the window.

"My Lord." Loretta's voice had become hushed. "You know who that looks like? I don't believe this. My Lord."

Katie put her hand over her mouth. Loretta kept saying, "I don't believe this." Katie's mind didn't believe it either, but her heart knew better. It went completely crazy.

She whispered, "Cole," and began to shake. She moved in a kind of trance, down the stairs and out the front door.

Other people were coming out of their houses too; word was spreading fast that Cole Grayson was riding through the neighborhood on a big black horse.

Diablo's hooves rang loudly on the hard brick street. He came at a steady trot, while Cole sat his back with style and grace, looking neither left nor right. He wore Levis and blue chambray, a dirty gray hat pulled low on his forehead. His jaw looked lean and hard. Directly in front of Katie he stopped and sat looking down at her. His eyes held the purposeful golden glare of a hunting eagle.

Katie just stared back at him, both hands clasped across her mouth. In one fluid motion Cole dismounted. He came slowly toward her, moving with his distinctive Cole Grayson walk, reaching one hand up to tilt his hat back.

"Katherine," he murmured, and waited.

"Cole." Katie cleared her throat, and said raspily, "What—?"

"One hero, ma'am; at your service."

Something bubbled up inside her and erupted in a gasp as he swept her into his arms—a gasp that was echoed by the crowd that had gathered to watch.

Katie whispered hoarsely, "Cole, what in the world are you doing?"

"Rescuing a damsel in distress," he said with a growl. "What does it look like?"

Incredible joy, wonder, and awe flooded through her on a silvery ripple of laughter. "I'm not in distress."

"You were the last time I saw you."

"Oh . . . Cole." His voice was harsh, his eyes so fierce, so intense. But the skin around them looked fragile and bruised, and the lines around his mouth were deeply etched. She touched them with her fingertips and felt them flow gently into a smile. Her heart swelled, filling her chest.

"Hang on tight," Cole rasped in her ear. "It's been a long time since I've had to pull off a stunt like this in front of a live audience."

"You can do it. Heroes can do anything," Katie whispered, shaking with love and laughter, then buried her face in Cole's neck and hung on for dear life while he put his foot in the stirrup, took a firm grip on both her and the saddle horn, and swung them both up onto Diablo's back.

The crowd cheered. Katie murmured, "The stuff legends are made of. Except—" She gazed up into his face and touched the brim of his battered hat. "I always thought heroes were supposed to wear clean white hats and ride white horses. Cole, a black horse named *Devil?*"

"I thought you said a hero is in the eye of the beholder. Woman, what you see is what you get."

"I'll take it." Katie sighed, putting her head on Cole's shoulder. He made a clicking sound with his tongue, and Diablo began to move through the applauding crowd at a parade walk. When they were clear of most of the spectators, Cole urged the big black into a trot, then a sedate canter. "Where are you taking me, sir?" Katie gulped, hanging on to Cole's neck.

"Where would you like to go, m'lady?"

Breathlessly she whispered, "Can we go to the mountains, Cole? I know a meadow where the sun comes up like the Fourth of July. . . ."

She felt his lips graze her temple, then soften with his smile. "That meadow's under about twenty feet of snow, darlin'. Might be a little rough on poor old Diablo."

"In that case," Katie said, tucking kisses into the opening of his shirt, "just take me someplace where I can hold you, kiss you. Oh!" She pressed her face into his warm front.

"What's the matter?"

"I just remembered! I've been eating taco dip all morning! Onions! Oh, damn. Cole—"

Diablo came to a jolting halt. Cole's arms rearranged themselves around her, and his head came between her and the sky. His mouth caught hers in mid-protest and tasted it thoroughly. Long before he was through, Katie had forgotten all about taco dip and onions, and things like gravity, and breathing.

"Woman," Cole said, growling, "you have some funny ideas about what's important."

"Me!" Katie's voice was weak, shaken. "You're the one who threw away the best offer you ever got and ran away to the other side of the world! How dare you come back here out of the clear blue sky and think you can sweep me off my feet—" She was struggling—unwisely, perhaps, considering the precariousness of her position—pounding on Cole's back with her fists. "Come to think of it, I don't want to go anywhere with you! *Put me*—"

Cole just laughed, and silenced her in the best possible way. When she was limp and thoroughly breathless, he said, "Now, hush," and nudged Diablo into a trot.

The traffic light at Pacific Coast Highway was with them; they crossed without so much as a pause, then proceeded on across parking lots and bike paths to the beach. When they reached the firm sand at the edge of the water, Cole urged Diablo into a gallop.

The beach was all but deserted, and the few surfers

and fishermen paid them no mind. Diablo's hooves made a flat sound on the sand and light, skipping splashes in the waves. Disconcerted sea gulls screeched at their passing. A dog barked. The thunder of the breakers rolled and receded. Katie's hair came loose and the wind caught it and blew it across Cole's face. Diablo's hoofbeats went on and on, racing the wind and the waves.

Far down the beach, where the nearest houses perched high on cliffs, jagged rocks spilled across the sand and into the ocean. Here the waves met the rocks with a sound like timpani, sending spray high over the rocks, leaving tide pools filled with sea urchins and starfish and tiny scuttling crabs. Here Cole pulled Diablo to a halt and dropped his reins to the sand. He eased Katie out of his arms and set her feet carefully on the ground, then swung himself out of the saddle. When he ducked under Diablo's neck, she was standing a little way off, with her back to him, rubbing her arms. He stood for a moment watching her, feeling his heartbeat in his throat, then went to her and put his arms around her and pulled her gently back against him.

"Katherine, I know I hurt you." His voice was raw with the awareness of her pain. "I don't really know what I can say to you except that I think I know, now, what's important to *me*. And what isn't. I don't know what took me so long. I guess I just couldn't believe I was really going to get another chance. But when I left you . . . it wasn't so much that I missed you, as it was that part of *me* was missing. So I came home to try and find it. And I read your book. And there were all my missing pieces. And they were all *you*." It was impossible to say anything more for a while, so he just stood still and held her, feeling her body tremble. After a time, when he could talk again, he said, almost fearfully, "Katherine? I think you could hold me now, if you still want to."

She turned in his arms, not in a rush, but slowly, stiffly, as if every part of her body hurt. She put her arms around him and laid her face against his chest and whispered, "Oh, Cole."

He held her almost awkwardly, rubbing her back. After some time he said huskily, "Katherine, is there any chance that offer of yours is still open?"

He felt her nod. "Of course it is, you idiot."

Joy warmed him like sunshine on a cold morning. He cleared his throat. "Just one thing—I can't accept your terms."

"What terms?" She sniffed and looked up at him.

"You said all you needed was for me to let you love me. I'm afraid I'd have to insist on loving you back. Could you handle that?" She nodded slowly, not taking her eyes from his face. "And another thing—this hero business. Reading that book, I found out that I've been taking myself and my damned image too seriously. I think I'd like to forget all about—" He stopped, because she was shaking her head.

"No," she said fiercely. She reached up to touch his face. There was a light in hers, something radiant, something that carried the sunshine clear to the center of his heart. "Cole, I don't care what anyone else thinks. You'll always be a hero . . . to me."

And that, Katie thought as she lifted her face for his kiss, was as it *should* be.

THE EDITOR'S CORNER

In celebration of our first anniversary we printed the following in our Editor's Corner—"It seems only a breathless moment ago that we launched LOVESWEPT into the crowded sea of romance publishing." Many things have happened in the years since we published the first LOVESWEPTs. The market has seen the birth of new romance lines and, sad to say, the demise of romance lines. Through it all we have remained true to the statement we made in our first anniversary issue—"Each time we've reached the goal of providing a truly fresh, creative love story, we find our goal expands, and we have a new standard of freshness and creativity to strive for." We try. Sometimes we don't hit on the mark. Sometimes we astonish even ourselves by hitting it square in the center. But thanks to the support of each of you, all the LOVESWEPT authors are growing and learning, while doing what we most like and want to do. We have even more of a challenge in presenting not just four, but six terrific romances each month.

It is such a pleasure to have a Helen Mittermeyer love story to kick off our expanded list next month. In **KISMET,** LOVE-SWEPT #210, Helen gives you another of her tempestuous romances with a heroine and hero who match each other in passion and emotional intensity. Tru Hubbard meets Thane Stone at one of the most difficult times in her life—certainly not the time to fall head-over-heels in love. Yet she does, and it looks as if she's rushing headlong into another emotionally disastrous situation, not just for herself, but for Thane, too. And so she runs as far and as fast as she can. But she's failed to realize her man is ready to walk through fire for her. A very exciting love story!

If there's a city more romantic than Paris, someone has failed to let me know. I think you'll love the setting almost as much as the heroine and hero in Kathleen Downes's LOVESWEPT #211, **EVENINGS IN PARIS.** From the moment Bart Callister spies a lovely mystery woman on the deck of the Eiffel Tower until he has pursued and caught lovely Arri Smith there's breathless, mysterious love and romance to charm you. But Arri's afraid. She knows she's no siren! You'll relish the ways that Bart handles her when she thinks *all* her secrets have been revealed. A true delight!

It is a great pleasure for me to introduce you to our new author Margie McDonnell and her poignant romance **BANISH THE DRAGONS,** LOVESWEPT #212. I had the pleasure of working with Margie before I came to Bantam, so I know she writes truly from knowledge of the heart and of courage, traits

(continued)

that she shows in her own life. Here she brings you a captivating couple, David and Angela, who know the worst that life has to offer and whose bravery and optimism and head-over-heels love will make you sing for joy, when you're not cheering them—and the children they deal with in a very special summer camp. A truly heartwarming, memorable debut.

Sit back, relax, and prepare to chuckle with glee and thrill to romance as you read Joan Elliott Pickart's **LEPRECHAUN**, LOVESWEPT #213. Imagine Blake Pemberton's shock when, home sick with the flu, a woman appears at his bedside who is so sprightly and lovely she seems truly to be one of the "little people" of Irish legend. And imagine Nichelle Clay's shock when she shows up to clean an apartment and confronts a sinfully gorgeous hunk wrapped in one thin sheet! A charming romp, first to last.

Welcome back Olivia and Ken Harper with **A KNIGHT TO REMEMBER**, LOVESWEPT #214. Tegan Knight sizzles with surprises for hero Jason Sloane, who is sure the T in her first name stands for Trouble. She'd do just about anything to thwart his business plans, but she hadn't counted on his plans for her! And those she cannot thwart—but what red-blooded woman would even want to? Two devilishly determined charmers make for one great romance.

LOVING JENNY, LOVESWEPT #215, showcases the creativity and talent of Billie Green. There are very few authors who could pull off what Billie does in this incredible story. Her heroine, Jenny Valiant, crashes her ex-husband's wedding reception to inform him their quickie divorce was as valid as a three dollar bill. Then she whisks him away (along with his bride) to sunny Mexico for another, but this time valid divorce, and sweeps them all into one of the most tender, touching, humorous romances of all time. A fabulous love story.

Enjoy!

Carolyn Nichols

Carolyn Nichols
Editor

LOVESWEPT
Bantam Books, Inc.
666 Fifth Avenue
New York, NY 10103

NEW!
Handsome Book Covers Specially Designed To Fit Loveswept Books

Our new French Calf Vinyl book covers come in a set of three great colors—royal blue, scarlet red and kachina green.

Each 7" × 9½" book cover has two deep vertical pockets, a handy sewn-in bookmark, and is soil and scratch resistant.

To order your set, use the form below.

HANDSOME, SPACE-SAVER
BOOKRACK

ONLY
$9.95

- hand-rubbed walnut finish
- patented sturdy construction
- assembles in seconds
- assembled size 16" x 8"

Perfect as a desk or table top library— Holds both hardcovers and paperbacks.

Nevco US Pat. 3,464,565
